MEMOIRS OF A GUARDIAN ANGEL

Memoirs of a Guardian Angel

Graham Downs

Published by Graham Downs

5 May 2018

Published 5 May 2018 by Graham Downs, at http://www.lulu.com/

Memoirs of a Guardian Angel, first published 6 April 2018 (E-pub ISBN: 978-0-620-78888-5 / Smashwords E-pub ISBN: 978-0-620-79350-6 / Amazon Kindle ASIN: B079Z9BG9B)

This edition ISBN 978-0-620-79709-2 (Paperback Edition)

https://www.grahamdowns.co.za/

Table of Contents

Memoirs of a Guardian Angel

PART I

Graham Downs

Memoirs of a Guardian Angel

Chapter One

People often say they have a guardian angel looking out for them, especially when they survive a harrowing experience, like almost crashing their cars, falling off ladders, or choking on pieces of chewing gum. After a near-catastrophe like that, how often have you thought, "Wow, my guardian angel must be really looking out for me today?"

But I wonder how many people actually believe it to be true. There aren't many people who talk openly about their guardian angel when things are going well... are there?

My name is Adam, and I am a guardian angel.

I don't recall much about my life on Earth. I have no memory of who I was or how I died. But what I do remember, is that I was one of those people who truly believed that guardian angels existed. When I died, I discovered the truth: not only do they exist, but there is a whole administrative division in their world, dedicated to their management and training.

Upon my arrival, I was greeted by a burly, balding man with a round face and a white robe. He introduced himself as Peter.

"Hold on," I said. "Why are you human? I thought everyone up here wore halos, had wings, played the harp, and shone with light."

Peter chuckled. "I get that a lot. First of all, contrary to what you humans believe, this is not 'up here'. This is the World Beyond the Veil, and it exists more-or-less adjacent to the world you were occupying a few minutes ago."

Up until that point, I hadn't really thought about it. I was dead. Of course, I was dead. And this was Heaven. Peter. The Pearly Gates. The whole shebang. I tried to remember what had led me here, or where I was before. I had nothing. It wasn't as if my memory was a blur. It just wasn't there.

I choked back tears and ran my fingers through my hair. "H-how did it happen?"

"I'm not at liberty to say." Peter pursed his lips and exhaled loudly. "Now if you'd please stop interrupting me."

"Sorry. Please go on."

"Where was I? Oh, yes, the reason I appear so human is that I'm the first being you people see when you arrive, and we need to make your transition as comfortable as possible. You humans have no idea how things really work, and if the first thing you saw was me as I truly am, you'd never be able to handle it. Those beyond this gate appear quite different, but also not what you'd expect. There are no halos, no wings, no shining light, and no harps." He pointed to his long white beard. "At least I have this, though. That's something, right?"

I gasped, still unable to comprehend what was happening. And why couldn't I remember anything?

Peter continued. "The beings you will meet on the other side of this gate look more like translucent blue outlines. It's difficult to explain, but that's actually what you look like now, too."

I looked at my hands and saw what he meant. The outline of my fingers was very pronounced, but my hands themselves were blue glass. Through them, I could see the ground. And then I noticed one more thing—the ground didn't look like any ground that I was used to. It was puffy, white, and cushiony. If I shifted my weight, it was almost like I was standing on a jumping castle.

I felt like I was going to pass out. I was shaking like a leaf.

Peter placed his hand on my shoulder. "There, there. It's all a bit much at first, I understand. But if you'll just go through that gate, everything will be fine." He studied the clipboard, resting on a lectern in front of him. "Hmm. Interesting. You're meant to speak to John about being a guardian angel. Just ask for him when you get to the other side. He'll explain everything you need to know."

I was meant to speak to *whom*? About *what*?

I opened my mouth to speak, but before I got to say anything, the huge golden gates behind him parted of their own accord. "Well, hurry along then. We can't stand out here, chatting for the rest of eternity."

Just as Peter promised, the world beyond the gate didn't look anything like the world outside it. It didn't look anything like the human world, either.

For one thing, there seemed to be no ground. If I looked down, the puffy white cushiony stuff was gone, to be replaced with nothing. Below my feet was a black void. If I bent down and tried to touch it, I couldn't—my hands dangled below my feet and I felt nothing but air. I could touch the soles of my translucent blue shoes without losing my balance.

There were many beings ("people", for want of a better word) in this void, but I saw nothing that could be considered a landmark. Just inky blackness punctuated with these translucent creatures. They were distinguishable from each other by the outlines of their faces and hair-line drawings, filled in with glassy blue. I presumed they were angels.

The creatures were all hurrying to-and-fro, I guessed busy with whatever it was that angels did.

I was about to find out just what that was because when I looked again, one of them was walking purposefully towards me.

"Hi," he said, extending out his hand. "I'm John. You must be Adam; I've been expecting you. You're going to be a guardian angel."

What struck me the most was that I didn't quite hear him with my ears. I saw the blue outline of his lips moving, but the sound of his voice sort of materialised in my head. When Peter had spoken outside the gates, I'd heard him in the *normal* way. That must be something else they do to help us recently departed adjust.

Thinking of that made me choke up again, but I swallowed back the tears and took his hand. I was about to respond when he cut me short. "No time for pleasantries. Let's get moving. The first day of training has already started."

John had high hopes for me as a guardian angel because not many humans actually believed in them. When I was alive, I'd been one of the few who had. He said that was the first obstacle conquered already.

The training consisted of a group of us sitting in a room. Things approximating chairs were arranged to face a large screen. Not that I think we needed either the chairs or the screen, but I think it was a bit easier for us to imagine it that way. We sat on the chairs as John showed us images of various guardian angels in action, at various places and various points in time on Earth.

John said that we could be sent anywhere, at any time. In fact, he went on, time—as we knew it when we were alive—didn't exist here. When we were alive, we were taught to see it as a continuous line, with a past, present, and future. Here, it was more like a ball of wool, and at any point, one could take a pinch of it and visit Earth's history at the time represented by that pinch.

"But what about the future?" asked one of my classmates.

"The future is a bit too complicated for that analogy," replied John. "If you could imagine that each of those pinches of wool where actually another ball, you might come close to understanding. There are an infinite number of possible futures, and there's no telling with any certainty which one will come to pass. We guardian angels don't often concern ourselves with it, though. We're there to help the people who live and have lived."

At one point, I looked up at the screen and saw a female guardian angel, sitting in a ghostly armchair with her hands rested on the arms, and a determined expression on her face. On her head was one of those old-timey open-faced crash helmets, and the whole contraption rested on the roof of a car going at considerable speed down a road.

"Who is *that*?" I pointed at the screen.

"Oh, that's Liz," replied John. "She likes to show off. Right now, she's in the year twenty-sixteen, protecting the driver of that car, a bit of an accident-prone woman who's had three near-misses on the road in as many months."

While he was speaking, a car on the opposite side of the road veered out in front of Liz. The angel leaned to the left, and the car she was protecting coasted out of the way, narrowly avoiding a head-on collision. The woman driving the car pressed her hooter, and the other car flashed its headlights angrily. We all applauded the ease with which Liz had averted disaster.

"There's another thing you ought to know," said John. "When you're out there, in the field, nobody else can see you. Some sensitive humans, like Adam was, might be able to feel your presence, but that's it. You also won't see any other angels. They're there, of course, some of them protecting other humans yours comes into contact with, but they can't see you either."

"What will our first mission be like?" asked the student who'd asked about the future.

"That, I can't say. None of us chooses our assignments, and none of us chooses when they're finished. In fact, when your training is finished, you will simply disappear from here without warning, and we'll be able to find you using the monitor."

As it happens, I was the first person to "graduate".

A few weeks later, I was sitting with the other students, watching a guardian angel on the screen, when I started to feel dizzy.

I stood up and pressed my hand against my head, and then all at once, it felt as though my insides were coming up through my throat. Not that I had insides anymore, and no throat either, for that matter, but if I had had insides, and I had *had* a throat, that's what it would've felt like.

I pressed my hands over my mouth, trying to suppress the unbelievable urge to vomit.

The other students leapt from their seats and started running around, unsure of what to do. But John just stood there, watching and smiling.

A moment later, my world was spinning. Like some psychedelic spiralling pinwheel in a low-budget psychological thriller movie. The spiral grew, engulfing my whole vision, and kept spinning. Spinning, spinning, spinning.

And then it was spinning in the opposite direction, unwinding itself.

Eventually, it disappeared.

The world I now gazed upon was not the world it had been. It was a room. Just an ordinary room, with a beige carpet on the floor, and a television set against the wall. Looking around, I saw a green lounge suite—a single chair with a double and triple couch. The walls were painted eggshell, and on the floor, I saw a girl. A human girl, with brown hair in pigtails.

She was kneeling on the ground, pushing a small plastic fire engine, making vroom vroom noises.

I heard a voice, coming from somewhere else in the house. "Rebecca, baby! Come on, it's time to go wash your hands."

Chapter Two

So that was to be my first assignment.

Rebecca Martin.

A three-year-old girl.

Sounds simple enough. I mean, how much trouble can a three-year-old girl get herself into, right?

Rebecca's mother, Jane, perched her on her lap during lunch, dished up a small portion of food, and chatted with her daughter as she fed it to her. She was plainly a kind and caring mother.

The girl yammered on in that toddler's voice that only a mother can understand. First, she told her mom how much fun she'd had playing with her fire engine, then about the songs she'd sung and the pictures she'd drawn in nursery school...

And then I realised that I could understand every word she was saying, perfectly.

She yawned, and her mother told her to put her hand in front of her mouth when she did that.

"I'm bored," I thought I heard her say. "I hope mommy lets me go soon. I want to go play."

But her lips hadn't moved. And that's when it hit me, and it made perfect sense. It wasn't so much that I could understand what she was saying; it was that I could hear everything she was thinking.

When Jane finally let Rebecca go, and lifted her off her lap and onto the ground, the girl ran off excitedly.

I took a moment to survey the kitchen. There was a blue plastic table in the centre of the room, with four steel-and-plastic chairs around it. The floor was a black-and-white chequerboard pattern.

The back door was open, and Rebecca was heading straight for it.

"Rebecca, sweetie, watch out for that..."

And then time stopped.

I could see the poor girl, suspended in mid-step, her right foot in the air, about to make contact with the ground. The ground that wasn't there. In her haste, Rebecca had forgotten about the rather high step just outside the back door. If I didn't act soon, she would tumble down it, and that could do some serious harm.

I lunged forward, between her and the open doorway, and shoved her in the chest.

Time started again.

Rebecca fell backwards, just as her mother was on her feet, running towards her daughter, who fell flat on her bottom.

The girl looked up, and slowly her playful grin turned into a frown. She screamed blue murder.

Jane picked her up, and held her close, "There, there. Did you fall on your bum? Don't worry, you'll be fine." She sighed. "That could've been a lot worse."

Rebecca looked up at her mom, pouted her lips, and said, clear as anything, "Shit!"

Jane's eyes went wide. I thought she was angry, but all at once, she burst out laughing. "Rebecca," she tried to sound stern. "I don't know where you heard that word, but I don't ever want to hear you say it again. That's a bad word." She wagged her finger in front of Rebecca's face, but then she hugged her daughter again and said, "I'm really glad you're okay, though. You'd better thank your guardian angel for that one."

Even though I knew it was only an expression, I beamed with pride. I screamed, "Yes! Yes, that was me!"

But of course, Jane didn't hear me. Jane didn't even know I was there.

But something strange happened: Rebecca stopped crying, sniffed, and looked directly at me. She let out a giggle.

"Can you see me?" I asked, but she just turned away again, and buried her face in her mother's chest.

Later that day, Rebecca was sitting on Jane's lap in the lounge, watching cartoons. The child was giggling hysterically at the antics on the screen, while Jane was nodding off.

I was beginning to wonder where Rebecca's father was in all of this when I heard a car door slam outside.

Rebecca heard it too. She leapt up from the couch. "Daddy!" she yelled, running towards the front door. Jane smiled thinly, wiped her brow, and slowly got to her feet.

By the time Rebecca got to the door, the key was in the lock, and I could hear it turning, the other keys jangling on the keyring.

The door opened, and a man stepped through. He looked older than Jane, and wore a suit with the top button undone and a tie pulled loose. He needed a shave, but the black hair on his head was cut short.

"Becca!" he said, as he picked up his daughter, and hugged her tight.

He glanced over at Jane. "Hey, babe. How was your day?"

"Hi, Mark. It was fine, thank you. Why are you in such a good mood?"

"No reason." He kissed Rebecca on the head. "Just a good day at work. And I couldn't wait to come home to my two favourite girls."

Rebecca giggled.

Jane rolled her eyes and left the room.

I'm so glad daddy's in a good mood today, thought Rebecca. I don't like it when he's upset.

This thought-reading thing was going to take some getting used to.

That night, Rebecca had begged her parents to let her sleep in her own room. Jane was apprehensive, but Mark agreed eagerly, saying it would give him some quality time with his wife. Finally, Jane acquiesced.

I was standing over Rebecca, tucked into bed, under her Hello Kitty duvet with her head resting on her Hello Kitty pillow. She was awake and staring straight at me. I knew she couldn't see me, but I was convinced that she could sense me.

There were low mumbles coming from her parents' room next door. I couldn't make out what they were saying, but I knew Rebecca could hear them too.

After a few moments, a word could be clearly heard: "Bitch!"

Then, a slightly lower voice, but still discernible. "Keep your voice down, Mark. You'll wake Rebecca."

Rebecca started grizzling. I heard her thoughts. *Why does it always happen? Don't mommy and daddy love each other?*

"*I'll* wake Rebecca?" Mark raised his voice a bit more. "That's rich, coming from you. You started it! Why do you have to be so damn cold all the time?"

"I'm not cold 'all the time'. You got sex just the other day. I'm not a machine, you know."

Rebecca stopped grizzling. She went deathly silent, wide eyes staring at the ceiling, and she pulled her duvet up under her chin.

Her parents' bedroom door slammed open, and I heard the stomping of feet down the passage. Then the front door slammed open and closed. A short while later, I heard faint sobs through the wall adjoining the two rooms.

Memoirs of a Guardian Angel

"Rebecca," I asked, "does daddy ever hit mommy?"

If she heard me, she didn't show it. She just pulled the duvet up higher and stared at the ceiling with those wide, terrified eyes.

The mood was cold the next morning at breakfast. Rebecca sat next to Jane at the kitchen table, rubbing milk and cereal all over her face, while Jane tried unsuccessfully to feed her.

Mark came into the room shirtless and unshaven, scratching under his arm. He'd arrived home late last night, drunk, and fallen into bed next to Jane.

Nodding at his wife and daughter, he grunted and opened the cupboard to retrieve a bowl. He set it down hard on the counter, grabbed the box of cereal and poured himself a helping. After opening the fridge and taking out the box of milk, he sloshed some into the bowl. The kitchen chair grated on the linoleum floor as he pulled it out, breaking the silence in the room. He sat down.

"Aren't you going to put the milk back in the fridge?" asked Jane.

Mark got up with a huff and made a dramatic showing of opening the fridge, returning the milk, and closing the door. He bowed theatrically and sat back down at the table and took himself a spoon off the cutlery rack.

Jane stared blankly at him and shook her head. "Why aren't you dressed? You're going to be late for work."

"Going in later," said Mark, through a mouthful of cereal. "Got a late meeting."

"Well, we need to get going, or Rebecca's going to be late for school." She stood up and took Rebecca's hand. "Come along, baby." Jane leaned in to kiss Mark, but he turned his cheek. She clenched her fists in frustration, but kept her voice even. "Well, since you're leaving later, would you mind clearing up?"

When Mark didn't respond, Jane walked Rebecca to the door, opened it, and dragged her out.

"Bye, daddy!" said Rebecca.

Daddy just nodded.

It turned out that Jane was a teacher at a Primary School not far from where Rebecca went. Her hours made it easy to drop her daughter off in the mornings, and pick her up on the way home.

Rebecca was still distraught about her father, but she was a brave girl. She didn't say anything about what had happened last night or this morning. It was a short drive to her nursery school, and she chatted along about all the things that she was going to do today.

When they arrived, Jane went to the back and unbuckled Rebecca's car seat. As she was lifted out of the seat, Rebecca didn't whine or sniffle, and her mother even had to remind her to give her a kiss.

She struggled her way out of her mother's arms, yelled "Bye, mommy!" and ran into her teacher's waiting arms.

Katie beamed when Rebecca arrived. She leant forward and put her hands on the tops of her knees. "Good morning, Rebecca! How are you today?"

"Good!" replied Rebecca, and gave her teacher a big hug around the waist.

"I'm glad. Come along. Let's go inside, and join the other children."

Some of the others had already arrived and were sitting on the floor in a circle, waiting for the rest of the kids.

I really like school, thought Rebecca. *I hope daddy's okay.*

After everyone was settled, Katie announced story-time.

She pulled up a chair and sat in the circle. The children gathered around.

Katie started telling her story, about three little pigs. It had something to do with houses, and a wolf blowing them down, but Rebecca wasn't really paying attention. She kept thinking about her dad, who didn't even say goodbye to them this morning. She wondered if she'd done something to upset him. If he didn't love her anymore.

All of a sudden, Katie stopped talking. The children were pointing at Rebecca and giggling.

It pains me to admit, I was too caught up in Rebecca's thoughts to notice what had happened. Rebecca looked down at her crossed legs, to see a puddle of urine on the floor between them. Once she realised what she'd done, she went red in the face and burst into tears.

Katie wasted no time getting up from her chair and picking Rebecca up. She held her close and cooed. "Aw, did we have a little accident? Don't worry, Rebecca. It happens to everyone, and people shouldn't laugh at you." She scowled at the other children, who stopped laughing and looked away sheepishly. "Now, let's see if mommy packed you some spare clothes."

She had. Katie took Rebecca into the bathroom, and changed her. Soon, Rebbecca was giggling playfully again, and the whole incident was forgotten.

Cut-and-stick time. The children giggled playfully to themselves as they cut magazines to ribbons.

Rebecca was cutting a picture of a model, from an article about obesity and eating disorders. Of course, she didn't know what the article was about since she couldn't read. She was just thinking it was a pretty lady, who looked a bit like mommy.

There I was, getting sidetracked again. I forced myself to snap out of it, just in time to see Rebecca's head roll forward, a smidge too much. She held the scissors in her right hand, pointing upward, and if I didn't do something soon, she would poke her eye out!

Just like what had happened in the house the previous day, time froze. This time, I wasn't surprised. Quickly, I moved forward, grabbed the scissors out of her hand, and threw them on the table. I restarted the clock (so to speak), and Rebecca punched herself in the eye.

For a moment, it seemed as though time had frozen all over again. Rebecca looked up, and her smiling lips slowly curled downward. Then she burst into tears.

"Oh dear, Rebecca's really in the wars today, isn't she?" Katie rushed over and put her arm around her shoulders. "There, there. It's all right. No harm done. Let's have a look at what you're busy with."

"No harm done" was right. Thanks to me. I was beginning to get a handle on this whole "guardian angel" thing, but I wasn't quite sure if I liked it. I breathed a sigh of relief.

When Jane arrived that afternoon to pick Rebecca up from school, she noticed that her daughter was in her spare clothes. Katie explained to her about the unfortunate accident.

Rebecca blinked at her mother with wide, apologetic eyes. "Sorry, mommy."

Jane clicked her tongue, feigning disappointment, but then she smiled lovingly. "That's okay, baby," she said as she picked her daughter up and cuddled her. "These things happen. That's why I send spare clothes. Let's just not make a habit of it, okay?"

Rebecca grinned happily. "Okay, mommy."

"Now, say goodbye to Katie. You'll see her tomorrow."

Rebecca gave her teacher a hug and a kiss on the cheek and waved goodbye as Jane carried her to the car.

"Mommy, when's daddy coming home?"

Rebecca was sitting on her mother's lap at the kitchen table. She'd not been very talkative during the ride home from school, giving only one-word answers when Jane had asked her what they got up to. I knew she was thinking about her dad. I tried to project positive thoughts into her head, to try to get her to cheer up, but none of it had worked.

Jane bit her lip. "He'll be home by five, baby."

"What's the time?"

Despite herself, her mother chuckled. She glanced at the clock on the wall. "It's half past four. Maybe it's time you learnt to tell time."

"Mommy, I'm only three!" Rebecca giggled, and Jane leaned in and tickled her tummy. That was probably the first time I'd seen her smile all afternoon.

Five o'clock came and went, and Jane decided they may as well eat dinner. She dished up a plate for Mark and put it in the warm oven. Then she and Rebecca sat down to eat, or rather to try and get Rebecca to eat.

Six o'clock came and went. Rebecca kept wondering where her father was. Each time she asked, Jane became more and more agitated. Eventually, she yelled, "Becca, I don't know!"

This caused Rebecca to burst into tears, and run to her room.

Since I am forced to go wherever my ward goes, I found myself standing there beside her.

I wish daddy were here, she thought. *Mommy will feel much better when daddy comes back.*

After a few moments, Rebecca realised nobody was paying attention. Her tantrum disappeared, and she shrugged and waddled into the lounge, sat down on the floor and picked up the doll she'd left there the previous day. She held it up and pretended it was a woman, making dinner.

At five past six, a car door slammed in the street outside. A moment later, the sound of a key rattling in the lock.

At the sound, Jane came back into the lounge.

When the door opened, Mark stumbled in, reeking of alcohol.

"Daddy!" cried Rebecca, and ran towards him with her arms outstretched.

He didn't acknowledge her. He just slurred, "Wheresh my dinner?"

"In the oven," replied Jane. "You're late. And drunk."

Mark waved her away, loped across to the kitchen and opened the drawer. "It's dry."

"Well, that's what you get when you leave food in a warm oven for an hour."

"You stupid bitch!" said Mark, as he lunged towards her. "I don't have to deal with this."

"Mommy!" screamed Rebecca, as massive tears rolled down her cheeks. She ran towards her parents, getting in between them.

If Mark saw her, he didn't care. He kicked her so hard that she landed on her butt and skidded across the floor. She screamed even louder.

Jane punched Mark in the face. He took a step back and looked at her incredulously, massaging his jaw. He didn't say a word.

Rebecca's mother got down on her haunches and cradled her daughter's face in her hands. She looked up at Mark.

"Get out!" she screamed.

Chapter Three

For ten years I stayed with Rebecca.

The first five of them were really difficult; the divorce had been long and messy, as divorces often are. Mark had kept the house, and Rebecca and Jane were forced to rent a much smaller one in the city. The previous year, when Mark had emigrated to Australia, Jane asked if this meant that they could have the house back, but out of spite, he'd refused, and sold it.

Rebecca's parents had tried hard to shield her, but of course, they'd failed. She knew more than they realised. More than she let on.

Now a pretty girl of thirteen, she was enrolled in Grade Eight at a public High School nearby. She had friends and got good marks. Not fantastic marks, by any stretch of the imagination, but good marks. She was a good kid.

She spoke to her dad every couple of months over the phone, and he sent her money for her birthday each year. She loved him, but would never forgive him for what he did to her mother.

One afternoon, in the car on the way home from school, Jane was very quiet.

Rebecca had gotten used to the annoying questions her mother would ask her every day (which, like a typical teenager, she'd answer with mono-syllables, if at all), but today, there was none of that.

She stared out the window at the bleak, grey buildings of the city passing by, and felt a pang for their old house in the suburbs. She knew her mother felt it too, but today, it was more than that. She looked over at her mom's hands, white on the steering wheel. Jane was staring straight ahead.

"Mom? What's wrong?"

Jane wore a vacant expression, her body shuddering.

"Did you know your father's getting married?"

Rebecca gasped. "Married? What? No! I didn't even know he had a girlfriend!"

"Neither did I," said her mother. "Apparently they've been in a relationship for two years. What else hasn't he told us?"

Rebecca didn't know what to think. Her hand went up to her breastbone, to suppress her shock. She didn't really remember much of when her father still lived with them—she was only three when he left—but she remembered the pain he'd caused her mother, and she remembered everything Jane had told her over the years.

Still, when he spoke to her over the phone, she always felt that he loved her. She never imagined he'd keep anything from her.

"He doesn't want me anywhere near the wedding," Jane continued. "But he really wants you there. He wants you to fly to Australia and stay with them. I told him you're too young, and I can't afford to send you anyway. He's not even prepared to help pay."

By this time, Jane was sobbing openly, her shoulders heaving. She was blinking furiously, trying to keep her eyes on the road.

When Rebecca got home, she immediately stormed into her room and shut the door. She collapsed on the bed, pulled out her cellphone, and sent her dad a WhatsApp message:

Hi, daddy. Will you call me, please?

She couldn't make international calls on her phone, and didn't have enough data for a Skype call, so an instant message was the best she could manage.

There was a faded picture of her and her parents on the bedside table. She studied it for a few moments. Her mom said it was taken when she was two. She couldn't remember that, but they looked so happy together. The phone rang, interrupting her thoughts. She picked it up.

Although I could only hear her side of the conversation, I picked up Mark's words as they registered in Rebecca's mind. He spoke sleepily: "Rebecca? What's wrong? Are you okay? Do you know what time it is?"

She did, but she didn't care. It was barely dawn in Australia, but truthfully, a part of her was hoping she'd wake her father.

"Mommy told me you're getting married."

Mark sighed down the phone. "Yes, baby, that's true. She's a wonderful lady. You'd like her."

"Mommy also told me you want me at the wedding."

"I do. Very much. I know Janine does, too. She really wants to meet you."

"How long have you known her?"

"Two years," admitted Mark nervously.

"So, before you moved to Australia." Rebecca had been doing maths in her head. She steadied her voice. "Why haven't I met her before?"

"That was her idea. She didn't want to confuse things between you, me, and your mother."

"And now you want me to come all the way to Australia. Leave my friends, my life. Miss school. Mommy says you won't even pay." Rebecca's voice was shaking now, and the tears were becoming almost impossible to choke back. I could tell by her thoughts that she was furious.

"Baby, money's tight. But we'd really love for you to come. I'm sure if you asked your mother, she'd make a plan. Will you come?"

Before Rebecca could answer, she heard a woman's voice on the other end of the line. A bit muffled, but unmistakable. "Love? Are you okay? Who's on the phone?"

Then, her father's voice. "It's nothing, baby. Go back to sleep."

Rebecca burst into tears. "I'll think about it," she screamed into the phone. She hung up and threw it onto the bed.

Rebecca wanted to throw her phone against the wall and see it smashed to pieces. But she imagined her mom's reaction. We're not made of money, she would say. Her phone wasn't the best on the market anyway, but if she broke it, she probably wouldn't get another one soon.

Instead, she picked it up, and gently placed it on her bedside table. Then she sat on her pillow with her back pressed against the wall. She hugged her knees and rocked back-and-forth as she sobbed.

A moment later, there was a knock on the door.

"Becca? Baby, are you okay?"

"Go away." Rebecca sniffed down tears.

Jane didn't go away. She gently pushed the door open and poked her head inside.

When she saw her daughter, she rushed into the room, jumped onto the bed, and threw her arm around Rebecca's shoulders.

"What's wrong?" she asked.

Rebecca's tears flowed like a waterfall.

"Mommy, it's daddy," she blubbered, as the words came pouring out. "He says his new girlfriend really wants to meet me, but he's had her since before he moved to Australia, so why didn't she meet me then? He says I must go to their wedding, but I've never even been out of the country, and he won't even pay, and how are we supposed to afford it?"

Jane rocked her daughter gently. "There, there. You shouldn't be worried about money, baby. Let me worry about that." She reached over and grabbed a tissue from the box on Rebecca's table and dabbed it under her daughter's eyes. "The question is, do you *want* to go?"

Rebecca sniffed. "I... I don't know," she said. But I knew that was a lie, and I read the truth in her mind. I also read that she was far more grown-up than her mother gave her credit for.

I'd rather die than meet the slut *that dragged him away from us.*

The next day, Mark phoned Rebecca many more times, but she didn't take his calls. Aside from the fact that she didn't want to speak to him, and didn't know how to tell him how she felt about the wedding, she was in class.

In fact, she zoned out of her entire maths period thinking about him. Her teacher spent most of the period trying to hold her attention, without much success.

Mostly, she was just cursing him and his new fiancé in her head. Who knew that a thirteen-year-old girl could have such a repertoire of grawlixes?

Her phone rang for at least the twentieth time during second break. She pulled herself away from her circle of friends, and picked it up.

"Dad, what the fuck do you *want*?"

"Rebecca, don't you ever use that word with me or your mother again!"

"I'll use whatever words I fucking want," Rebecca shot

back. "Don't test me, *daddy*."

This wasn't a battle Mark was going to win. He exhaled loudly and changed the subject. "I was just wondering—"

"If I'd thought any more about coming to your wedding? Yes, I have, and I'm still thinking. I'll let you know. Bye!"

I must admit, I thought that this was a bit harsh. But then I saw how frustrated she was with all the calls that day. She still had no intention of going to the wedding, but she didn't know how to tell him. He was still her father, after all, and she did still love him. She just wished he would stop pressuring her so much.

That afternoon in the car, Jane wanted to know if Rebecca had thought any more about going to the wedding.

"No, mom, I haven't."

Rebecca just wanted to be left alone. She didn't tell her mother about all Mark's phone calls that day; she thought it would only make the pestering worse. She hoped he wouldn't phone again while she was in the car.

"I know you don't want to think about it, Becca. But you really should."

Rebecca snapped. "I'll think about it when I'm ready to think about it, mom. Can we drop it, please?"

Jane muttered something to herself. She focused her vision squarely on the road in front of her and gripped the steering wheel tighter. The two drove home in silence as Rebecca stared into space.

When they got home, Rebecca marched straight to her room. Jane didn't try to stop her, but just shrugged as she stormed past.

She threw her school bag on the floor and climbed onto the bed. She sat cross-legged, put her hands on her knees, and took a deep breath.

I wish this whole situation would just go away!

Her phone rang from inside her pocket. She pulled it out and glanced at the screen. Mark.

She killed the ringer, let out a sob, and threw the phone on the mattress next to her.

After a few moments, she got up. I could hear the resoluteness in her mind, but there was so much anger there it was difficult to discern specific thoughts. Slowly, she opened her bedroom door and poked her head out. She heard her mother rattling around in the kitchen.

She exited the room and crept down the passage. Into her mother's room, and then into the master bathroom.

I was powerless to do anything, except be pulled along behind her by an invisible tether.

Once in her mother's bathroom, she opened the medicine cabinet and pulled out a razor. With some difficulty, she removed a blade from the plastic casing.

As I figured out what she was planning, I frantically projected thoughts into her mind: *No, Rebecca. No, don't do it!*

But my projections had no effect. I prayed that her mother would see her, but it was no use—the rattling from the kitchen continued as Rebecca crept back down the passage and into her room.

She got onto her bed, cross-legged as before. In her right hand, she held the blade, trembling. She rotated her left, exposing the delicate skin of her wrist. I could tell that she was watching, actually *seeing* the blood pulse through it.

I continued to project, trying to get her to stop. I kept hoping her mother would come in… or something, anything would make her put down that blade so that she could take a deep breath and just think for a moment.

She dropped her right hand, and the blade pricked the skin on her wrist. The trembling was getting worse, but I could see that she was resolved. She was going to do it. A tiny bit of blood welled under the blade and trickled down her arm.

Her phone rang, and she glanced down at the screen.

Mark.

Please, Rebecca, I prayed. *Please, just answer your phone!*

And then she picked up the phone. Thinking that if she was going to leave this world, she might as well say goodbye, she pressed the Answer button.

"Hello, daddy."

She was struggling to maintain her composure, and her father could obviously hear it in her voice.

"Becca, what's wrong. Where are you?"

"In my room. With a razor-blade in my hand. Daddy, I just want to say goodbye."

I'm not sure how her father responded to this because I was focusing all my energy on getting through to Rebecca. Willing her with every fibre of my being to notice me, to stop this silliness and put down the blade.

A miracle happened: Rebecca went slack-jawed, and her eyes grew wide. She dropped the phone on the bed—I could hear Mark's frantic voice coming through the speaker—and stared straight at me.

I hadn't felt that way since the night in her bedroom when she was three. It was as if she knew I was there.

Rebecca, I asked. *Can you hear me?*

There was no reaction.

Her bedroom door burst open, and her mother rushed in. When she saw the blade between Rebecca's fingers, she rushed to the bed and grabbed her daughter in her arms.

Memoirs of a Guardian Angel

Rebecca dropped the blade and burst into tears.

"Mom," she sobbed in between her heaving for breath, "I think I need to go to the wedding. I need closure."

I was amazed. Just how old was this girl?

Her mom burst into tears, too. "Oh, baby. It's okay. Whatever it takes, we'll get you there. I promise!"

I was beaming with pride, and ready to see Rebecca and her family through this next great adventure in her life.

And then, the strangest, and most frustrating, infuriating thing happened. That pinwheel appeared again before my eyes. Spinning and spinning. Filling my whole vision. I wanted to scream out, "No!" I wanted to scream that Rebecca needed me now, more than ever. I needed to stay. I *wanted* to stay.

Pretty soon, the pinwheel took up my whole vision. The sound, too—I'll never forget that sound. A ringing in my ears, that grew louder and louder, until the spinning pinwheel and the ringing were all I could think of, all I could focus on.

Suddenly the ringing stopped. For a split-second, all was silent. The pinwheel changed direction again and started unravelling itself. My insides once again turned upside down, and slowly the silence was replaced with the overbearing sounds of traffic—engines roaring, tyres screeching, hooters hooting. I felt the wind rushing through me.

At some point during all this, I must've closed my eyes, because my vision was black. When I opened them, I realised that Rebecca's world was no more.

Graham Downs

Chapter Four

I had no more time to reflect on Rebecca and what became of her.

I was lying on my stomach, on a roof of a car. It was a long red sedan, and my hands clutched the sides of it. I stared ahead of me, in time to see the car I was travelling in veer into oncoming traffic, and another car's headlights speeding towards us.

After checking to make sure there were no cars to the side of us, I leaned hard to the left, causing the car to shift back into its proper lane, and the oncoming vehicle to pass without incident—although its hooter did blare angrily.

If I still breathed, I would have exhaled a sigh of relief. I stuck my head down into the car (it passed through the roof as if there was nothing there) to see who I was meant to be babysitting this time.

It turned out to be a woman, about thirty years old, with wavy brown hair. Heavy metal music was blaring through the car's speakers. She clutched a cigarette between her fingers, which she puffed on frantically.

She was muttering to herself.

That stupid dick of a husband. I bet you he's high again. Good-for-nothing sonofabitch. I don't know why I stay with him.

Those thoughts kept running through her mind, over and over again.

I lifted my head back up through the roof. It occurred to me that lying here, clutching the roof of a car was, no way to travel. I imagined Liz, the angel whom I had seen sitting in her comfortable armchair, and wondered if I could do it. I closed my eyes, and imagined an over-sized wingback chair, white with a floral pattern. When I opened them again, I was sitting comfortably, my arms resting nonchalantly on the arms of the chair.

Much better.

I shifted my weight slightly to the left to avoid another head-on collision. This woman clearly wasn't the best driver in the world, I can tell you that.

As we pulled up to the woman's home, I was daydreaming about Rebecca. I wondered how she and her family were getting on. Would she be able to get to Australia to attend the wedding? What a pity the Powers That Be don't allow us angels to see our wards' lives through to the end.

The house was a semi-detached, with a face-brick front wall and a nondescript door, accessible by climbing a short flight of stairs. Homely, but not extravagant.

The woman, whose name was Eve Matthews, ascended the steps as she fumbled on her keyring for the right one. She inserted it into the lock and turned it.

I floated behind, and followed her into a dirty lounge. On the floor was a dishevelled green carpet, and the only chair in the room was a moth-eaten love-seat. Sitting in the love-seat was a man, lying back and staring blankly at a small colour television, which was playing an old game show. There was a rubber tube wrapped around his right arm, and a syringe lay casually in his left hand.

"Eve, baby," he groaned as she walked in the room. "Come over here and give the love of your life a kiss."

She walked up to him, but didn't kiss him. Instead, she slapped the syringe out of his hand.

"Aiden, you useless piece of shit! You're high again. When are you going to get off your ass and get yourself a job?"

"Ah, baby…" Aiden wrapped his arm around her waist and

pulled her close. "You know I love you. Come on, give your munchkin a kiss." He tried to kiss her on the lips, but she turned her cheek instead.

"Don't be like that, love," he slurred. "How about some nookie, huh?" He grabbed her hand and rested it on his crotch, through his grey chinos.

This time, she didn't resist. She clicked her tongue, cocked her head slowly in mock disbelief, and said, "What are we going to do with you?" She unzipped his fly and got down on her knees between his legs.

At some point during their love-making, they had moved to the bedroom. I won't relate all the grisly details (I admit I averted my eyes), but when they'd finished, they lay in bed, smoking a cigarette.

"Baby, you know I love you," Eve was saying, "and you know I'm no saint, but that junk's going to kill you. You've got to stop."

Aiden took a long drag on the cigarette and passed it to Eve. "Ja, maybe," he said. "Maybe I should give it up and go find a job."

There was a moment's silence. Aiden stared into the deep pools of Eve's eyes, and she stared back. It was beautiful.

Then Aiden's shoulders shook with laughter.

Eve punched her boyfriend hard on the arm. "Dick!" She got out of bed and threw on a tee shirt. "And to think, I got on my knees for you. I'm going to make myself a sandwich."

"Aw," yelled Aiden behind her. "Aren't you going to make one for your lovey?"

Halfway out the bedroom door, Eve turned her head and snapped, "Make it yourself, you lazy slob."

A few minutes later, Eve came out of their tiny kitchenette and into the lounge. She perched on the couch and tucked her legs underneath her, with the sandwich on a plate, balanced on her lap.

Absently, she picked up the television remote and pressed the Power button. She lifted the sandwich to her mouth and robotically took a bite as she tried to focus on what was on the screen.

Stupid-dumb moron. I don't know why I stay with him.

Because you love him, the internal conversation with herself went.

Maybe, but he's going to kill himself one of these days, and then where will I be? And even if he doesn't, he's going down, and he's going to take me down with him.

Eve realised that she had no idea what she was supposed to be watching. She picked up the remote and clicked off the TV. Her sandwich was finished by now, and she absently dusted crumbs off her shirt onto the plate.

She reached over and picked up her handbag, which she'd left on the coffee table earlier. Rummaging inside it, she found her phone and a spare packet of cigarettes. She lit one and scrolled through the contacts on her phone, stopping on Mom.

She pressed dial and waited a few seconds, before she heard a voice on the other end.

"Hi, baby! How are you?"

Eve burst into tears.

"Mom," she sobbed. "It's Aiden. He was high again, and —"

Her mom sighed. "Oh, Eve, how many times do I have to tell you that man's no good for you? I don't know when you're going to just wake up and leave him. When he's got himself killed? Or worse… arrested?"

Eve hung up. She couldn't deal with the "I told you so's"

right now. She loved Aiden, and that was that. No matter what her mother said.

She sighed contentedly, and made her way back to the bedroom.

She got to the bedroom to find Aiden lying on his side, the covers bunched up tightly around him, even though it wasn't cold. The bedside lamp was still on, and she could see him breathing. He was also snoring heavily.

Eve rolled her eyes.

I really should have made him something to eat. Now he's gone to sleep without any supper.

That internal conversation came again: *He's not worth your effort. I'm sometimes amazed he can breathe on his own, without needing permanent mouth-to-mouth.*

That image made Eve giggle, despite herself.

Still, I love him. He's my Aiden, and that's that.

She climbed into bed and pulled some of the covers off of him so that she could have some herself. He groaned incoherently. After switching off the light, she shuffled closer to him, and put her arm around his waist.

"Night baby. I'm sorry."

He didn't say anything, but emitted a loud snort. Then the rhythm of his snoring returned to normal.

Eve fell asleep smiling.

The next morning, Eve woke up early for work. Aiden was still sleeping, so she busied herself with her morning routine. I learnt from her surface thoughts that she was a nurse at the local clinic, and she was currently on day-shift.

After she'd finished getting ready and had eaten breakfast, she stuck her head through the bedroom door. Aiden was still sleeping.

He looks so peaceful. I really shouldn't wake him.

She had some time to kill, though, so she decided she would make him a cup of coffee. After she'd done that, she crept back to the bedroom and left the mug of steaming liquid on Aiden's bedside table. She shook him gently.

"Aiden, baby. I'm leaving for work. I made you coffee. Don't sleep too late and let it get cold."

Aiden rolled over and grunted. He wiped his eyes. "Thanks, babes", he said groggily. "Have a good day. I love you!"

Then he promptly fell asleep again.

Eve practically skipped out of the house. She kept thinking how lucky she was to have a man who loved her. So what if he had faults—didn't everybody?

Eve had a pretty uneventful day at work. She did her rounds, gave a child a sucker here, helped someone to the bathroom there, and even had time for some tea-room gossip with the other nurses.

Simone had a fight with her boyfriend the night before, about his habit of leaving the toilet seat up. Eve thought Simone had it good if that was her boyfriend's only fault. She didn't say it, though.

Sometime after lunch, Eve was checking Nita's blood pressure, and chatting happily. Nita was eighty-three and had a hip replacement the previous day. The old woman was in high spirits, though, talking about her son and how he would be coming to pick her up that afternoon. She asked about Eve's love-life, and before long Eve found herself singing Aiden's praises—although she didn't mention the drug problem.

Eve had just finished checking the gauge on the blood pressure monitor (one-thirty over eighty-two. Slightly on the high side, but no real cause for alarm) when the clinic's crash doors burst open. She muttered to Nita that she would be right back, and sneaked a peek down the passage.

Two paramedics, a burly man and a young woman, were pushing a crash-cart with a man on it.

"Possible OD!" the male paramedic yelled. "Can we get a doctor please?"

Doctor Wilson came running, with Simone in tow. "We'll take him. What's he had?"

The paramedics ran down the man's vitals while Simone and the doctor escorted them to an observation room.

Eve returned to Nita's side. "Sorry about that. Never a dull moment in this place."

Later that afternoon, Simone caught up with her in the tea-room. "Did you hear about that OD earlier?"

"I did," said Eve. "I was in with Nita. Good thing you were there. It sounded hectic."

"It was. Heroine. The poor guy shot up a bunch of the stuff. He didn't make it." Simone pulled a tissue out of her pocket and dabbed under her eye. "It hit me pretty hard."

Eve was stunned. She patted Simone on the shoulder. "It happens to all of us, babe. You go home and rest. You'll be okay."

But it was Eve who wasn't really okay. She couldn't shake the image of the man, lying on the crash cart.

What if that had been Aiden? I don't know how I could've lived with myself if that had been Aiden.

Graham Downs

Chapter Five

Eve drove home with a heavy heart and mixed feelings. She truly loved Aiden, and because of that, she knew that she couldn't ask him to change.

But the overdose patient that day had gotten to her. She realised that if Aiden didn't stop his ways, that could easily be him one day. Eve wasn't sure if she'd be able to handle that.

She drove home quickly, and twice I had to intervene to prevent an accident. I don't know who her angel was before me, but he must've been good, to have kept her alive this long.

As Eve pulled into their driveway, her heart sank. Parked in the street was a battered blue Polo hatchback, and the front door of the house was standing open.

Enrico, she thought. *Shit. That's all I need.*

I gleaned from her thoughts that Enrico was Aiden's drug dealer, and if he was here, Aiden was probably buying drugs.

Determined to put a stop to it, Eve jumped out of her car and slammed the door. She stomped up the steps, through the open front door, and walked inside.

In the lounge, she saw her fears realised. Aiden was sitting back on the couch, smoking. Enrico stood in front of him, talking excitedly and gesticulating wildly at packets of fine white powder, strewn all over the coffee table.

"Hey, babe." Aiden's face lit up as he noticed her. "How was your day? You remember Enrico, right?"

"Evie!" Enrico drawled, as he turned to face her. "Long time no see, girl. Your boy here's been telling me things. Good things. How've you been?"

Eve suddenly felt sick. She didn't know what was going on here, but she was sure it had something to do with Aiden buying drugs. What else could that white powder have been?

"I-I can't do this," she blurted out. She stormed up the stairs into the bedroom, and slammed the door behind her.

She threw herself onto the bed and wept into her pillow.

Much as I would've loved to stay and find out what was going on, I now knew that wasn't possible, so this time it wasn't a surprise when I found myself being pulled after Eve by some invisible, supernatural force.

I stood and watched her, sitting on the edge of the bed, sobbing fiercely.

Her thoughts were racing, difficult to pin down.

Stupid bloody idiot. Why? Why him? Why me? I'm the idiot. I can't stay with him. I love him. I have to stay with him. He needs help. I'm not strong enough. I have to be....

She balled her hands into fists, threw her head back, and screamed, "Why me?!"

Finally, she slammed her fists down into the bed and stared blankly at the floor. *He doesn't even have the courtesy to come see why I'm upset. Why do I spend so much time worrying about him?*

The door burst open, and Aiden danced into the room.

"Baby, guess what?" he said, completely oblivious to her pain, or even the tears running down her cheeks. "Enrico offered me a job. A real job, babes. For real money."

Eve sniffed and rubbed her eyes. Aiden still didn't seem to notice. "What job?" she asked.

"Enrico gave me some of his stock. He said I could sell it for him, and he'd give me ten percent of whatever I make."

The corner of Eve's mouth began to twitch, and then she cackled maniacally. She got up and marched towards him, causing him to step back to avoid being run over.

"Are you *insane*?" she screamed, punctuating each word

with a finger in his chest. "Selling drugs? Shit, Aiden, that has to be the dumbest idea I've ever heard. I... no, I can't do this. I can't go on like this." She walked to the cupboard and got out a suitcase. She threw it on the bed, wrenched it open, and started unpacking his clothes from the cupboard.

It seemed like this was the first time Aiden actually had an inkling that something was wrong.

"Uh, baby, what are you doing?"

"You," she said and pointed her finger at Aiden. "You need to get out. This is *my* house, my bed, and I will not spend one more night with you in it."

Aiden hung his head, looking utterly crestfallen. I actually felt sorry for the guy.

"But baby," he said. "This is a job. I'm finally getting off my ass and doing something. I thought you'd be happy."

"Well, I'm not," she snapped. Then she took a deep, slow breath, and continued. "Aiden, I love you. I really do. But I can't handle the drugs anymore. We had a patient at the hospital today, over-dosed on heroin. He didn't make it. I kept thinking, what if it was you?"

"Oh, baby, I'm so sorry." Aiden moved to put his arms around Eve, to comfort her. She pushed him away.

"No. Don't touch me. You need to move out. We need to be apart, and I can't be with you anymore. Not until you're off the drugs."

Aiden looked Eve in the eyes. For once, she thought, he looked completely sober. "Baby, I'm so sorry. I'll get off the drugs, I promise I will. But I can't leave. Not tonight, anyway. Where would I go?"

"You've made that promise before." Eve's heart was breaking, but she knew she had to be strong. "Okay, you can leave tomorrow. But you *will* leave. Tonight, you'll sleep on the couch."

After Aiden left the room, Eve got up and closed the door, as an extra barrier between the two of them. She lay on the bed, on her side, staring at Aiden's empty cupboard.

There was a metal safe set into the floor, where Aiden kept his revolver. She remembered when he'd first bought it, and how long it had taken him to get approved for the licence. Then he'd taken her to the firing range and taught her how to shoot it. Good times. Fun times. Before the needles had messed him up. As far as she knew, he hadn't taken out that gun in years. Hadn't even thought of it. She doubted he even remembered it was there.

Had she been too hard on Aiden, she wondered? Should she have let him sleep in their bed tonight? Would he really change?

Eve searched her heart for an answer to that last question, and all she could think of was that he probably wouldn't. The tears came again, and eventually, she fell asleep.

Since there was nothing for me to do and angels didn't sleep, I just stood there, watching her. This was a terrible burden that had been placed upon her heart, and I didn't know how to help her. I thought of willing her to wake, to go to Aiden, apologise and invite him to her bed, but I wasn't sure if that was the right thing to do. Something inside me knew that this was the best thing for her—and it was her I had to think about, now.

She was restless. Shortly after midnight, she woke up thirsty. I followed her to the kitchen. She hesitated at the door, listening to the sound of Aiden's loud snoring coming from the couch.

Listen to him. He's sleeping like a log. Here I am worrying myself sick, and he doesn't even care.

After opening the tap and pouring herself some water, she got back into bed, but struggled to sleep.

Memoirs of a Guardian Angel

She eventually drifted off at around four-thirty. I watched the digital clock tick past five-thirty in its bright red LED digits. That was her normal time to get up for work, but I felt sorry for her, so I stopped the alarm from going off.

When I finally allowed her to wake at six, it was with a start. I would have assumed her first thought would be about being late for work, but it wasn't. She jumped out of bed, and bolted to the lounge, to find the couch empty, with Aiden's blanket neatly folded over the back. On the seat was a note:

> I'm gone. I would have SMSed, but I didn't want to wake you. I'm sorry for everything. Will be around while you're at work to get my stuff.
>
> Love you,
>
> Aiden

When she'd finished reading the note, Eve threw herself into the couch and, clutching the piece of paper in her hands, she sobbed.

A few minutes later, her sobbing was interrupted by the SMS tone of her cellphone. Her heart leapt as she picked it up, thinking it might be Aiden. It wasn't.

> Where r u? Dr Wilson looking. Cant cover any longer. Soz.

The message was from Simone. *Shit*, she thought, looking at her watch. Work started an hour ago. *Oh well, life goes on.* She quickly sent a message back, promising to be at work within the next thirty minutes. Then she rushed back to the bedroom and threw on some clothes; No time to shower. Her sobbing had abated somewhat, but her eyes were still bloodshot, and she took the time to wash her face and hastily apply some mascara before leaving for work.

The whole drive to work, Eve was choking back tears. She kept thinking how she'd made a terrible mistake with Aiden last night. She imagined him lying in a ditch somewhere, with a needle sticking in his arm.

By the time she arrived at work, an hour and a half late, her mascara had run all down her face. No time to re-apply, she grabbed a few tissues from her handbag, spit on one, and tried to wipe it off in the rear-view mirror.

A minute later, and deciding that it would have to do, she walked into the hospital's front doors.

"Where have you been?" asked Simone, when she saw her. Then, noticing the mascara smears on her face, she dragged her into the tea-room. "Eve, what's wrong with you? What happened?"

Eve was about to make up some lie, when another nurse burst into the room.

"We need a crash cart in Ward 22B, stat!"

Oh no, that's all I need.

Ward 22B was Nita's ward. The old lady was supposed to be discharged yesterday. Why was she still here?

The next few minutes were a blur, as Eve and Simone rushed to Nita's bedside. Doctor Wilson was there a few seconds later, shouting orders. The three of them pumped the old lady so full of drugs in the space of five minutes... but then she flat-lined. Doctor Wilson administered CPR for a good ten minutes more, but in the end, he had to call it.

Eve exhaled deeply, as Doctor Wilson left the room. Simone put her hand on Eve's shoulder.

"I'm sorry," she said. "She was supposed to go home yesterday, but her son didn't arrive. Good thing, I think. Well, it would've been, if we'd been able to save her. Come, let's go have a smoke."

The two of them sat on a concrete bench, in the shade of the old oak tree in the clinic courtyard.

"I dunno, Simone," sobbed Eve as she took a drag on her cigarette. "I don't know how it happened. She was fine yesterday. All chipper and happy, and excited to go home."

Her friend gave her a hug. "I know, babe. Blood clots happen so quickly. No-one could have known."

Eve dried her eyes. "I know, and it's not the first time. It's just... oh, everything really. First last night, and now this."

"Yes, speaking of that, what the hell happened to you, Eve? You've never been late for work before, and your mascara was running. What's going on?"

With that, Eve broke down and sobbed bitterly. She told Simone all about what had happened the previous night, about Aiden's visitor and so-called "job", about her reaction when he told her, and about the message she'd found that morning.

"Oh, Simone," she finished, sobbing into Simone's shoulder. "What have I done? He could be lying in a ditch now, for all I know."

"It's okay." Simone patted Eve gently on the back. "I honestly think you're better off without him, Eve. All that loser was doing was dragging you down."

Just then, another nurse stuck her head outside.

"Simone," she said, then clicked her tongue

sympathetically when she saw the redness under Eve's eyes. "Doctor Crane's looking for you inside."

Simone stubbed out her cigarette. "I'd better go, babe. Are you going to be okay?"

Eve sniffed. "I think so."

Simone squeezed her shoulder. "All right, then. We'll talk later. You stay a while. Compose yourself."

Simone got up and went back inside, and Eve lit another cigarette.

After two drags, the door opened again, and Doctor Wilson stepped outside. He fished a packet of cigarettes out of his shirt pocket and popped one in his mouth.

"Hello." He coughed nervously. "Got a light?"

Eve handed him a lighter. He jacked up his smoke and handed it back.

"Thanks," he said.

Eve took it and nodded politely.

He noticed the tears drying on her cheeks. "Sad news about the lady in 22B, isn't it? I hear she was supposed to go home yesterday."

"Yes. Her name was Nita. I was with her yesterday. She was in good spirits. But her son never pitched. And now...."

The doctor mumbled. "Ja, it happens. But it never gets easier."

They smoked in silence for a few moments, before he spoke again.

"So," he pulled sheepishly at his collar. "I've been watching you for a while." He suddenly went beet-red in the face. "Oh dear, that makes me sound like some kind of creepy stalker. I'm not good at this."

He took a nervous puff on his cigarette, and despite herself, Eve giggled.

"Anyway," he went on. "I've been thinking. Would you like to have dinner with me tonight?"

Eve's mouth dropped open. Was this man seriously asking her out on a date? She hardly knew him. But on second thought, maybe Simone was right. Maybe she did need a change from Aiden. Besides, she would've gone home that afternoon, and done... what, exactly? Sit and brood over a man who didn't deserve her anyway?

"I'm sorry," said Doctor Wilson, interrupting her reverie. "How insensitive of me. You don't even know my name." He stuck out his hand. "Hi, I'm Dennis."

"Pleased to meet you." Eve took his hand and shook it. "I'm Eve. And you know what? I would love to go to dinner with you."

Dennis' face lit up. "Really? That's fantastic. Pick you up at seven?"

Graham Downs

Chapter Six

The rest of Eve's work day was uneventful. She would occasionally pass Dennis in the passages, and when she smiled at him, he blushed and returned with a sheepish grin of his own.

When she left work that afternoon, it was with a light and happy heart, but as she drove closer to home, she began to get nervous. By this time, I was getting used to her near-misses on the road, as she let her mind wander to thoughts of Aiden, where he could be, and what he might be doing.

She opened the door to their semi-detached house and stepped inside, half-expecting to see Aiden sitting on the couch with his belly falling out from under his brown tee shirt, a beer in one hand and the remote in the other.

But the couch was empty. On the coffee table lay a set of keys. She walked to the table and picked them up. Aiden's.

Choking back tears, Eve walked to their bedroom and opened Aiden's cupboard. It was empty except for the small safe bolted to the floor. Aiden's safe, where he kept his gun. She was about to open it but pulled herself away. Aiden was gone, and that was all that mattered.

Eve's tears were streaming easily down her cheeks now, but she wasn't quite sure whether they were happy tears or sad tears. He was gone. The man she'd given ten years of her life to, was gone.

Pull yourself together, dammit! She scolded herself. *Here you are, about to be picked up by a sweet, honest, hard-working man. Not the most handsome man in the world, but so what? He's a doctor. Didn't your mother always want you to be with a doctor?*

She giggled giddily at herself, then. It was only one date.

A much-needed distraction from her sad, sorry life. She didn't really expect it to go anywhere. Did she?

About forty minutes later, Eve was freshly showered, primped, and plucked. All the tangles had been brushed out of her hair, which she let hang loosely down between her shoulder blades. Her mascara was freshly re-applied, and she was determined not to cry it out again.

She sat on the bed staring into Aiden's empty cupboard. The doorbell rang. Standing up, she set her shoulders, said "Goodbye Aiden," and went to the door.

Standing in the doorway stood Doctor Dennis Wilson. His short brown hair had a neat part down the centre, and his thick round plastic-rimmed glasses added to his dorky grin.

It was weird to see him out of his doctor's scrubs. *He does clean up well, though,* thought Eve, *with his white long-sleeve button-up shirt and thin black tie.*

He shot out his arm, holding a mixed bunch of flowers. "These are for you."

"Thank you," said Eve, taking the flowers. "I'll just go put these in some water." She left him standing there in the open doorway.

In the kitchen, she rushed around opening cupboards. *Vases, vases, vases. Do we even have any vases in this house?*

Finally, she opened the cupboard under the sink and found what she was looking for. An opaque, pink, square vase. It was a bit small for the massive bunch Dennis had just presented her with, but it would have to do. Quickly, she put it in the sink, opened the tap and filled it with water. Then she unceremoniously dunked the bunch of flowers into it.

The rushed back to Dennis and was about to give an apology for taking so long, but he smiled and held out his arm. She slipped her hand through it, and they walked down the driveway to his car.

He opened the passenger door for her. Eve's heart soared as he helped her into the car and closed the door. Then he moved over to the driver's side and got in.

"All ready?" he said, turning the key in the ignition. "Let's go."

Dennis proved to be the perfect gentleman. He took Eve to an exquisite restaurant, with white tablecloths and high-back chairs.

He pulled out her seat for her and waited for her to sit down, and as he took his own seat, a violinist began to play on the stage.

Eve reflected how she'd never been to such an expensive place. She hoped it wasn't costing Doctor Wilson too much. Then she had a harrowing thought and hoped that he wasn't *expecting* too much in return, either.

A waiter came to ask if they would like anything to drink. Dennis asked for a bottle of their best Chardonnay and said they would like a few minutes to browse the menu.

Eve flipped through hers, gasping at the prices. Filet Mignon, Lobster, some dishes she couldn't pronounce. Dennis, who seemed to already know what he wanted, lounged back in his chair and stared at her.

"What?" She lifted her head from her menu and met his gaze.

His eyes flicked away. "I'm sorry. I don't know if anybody ever told you what a beautiful woman you are."

Now it was Eve's turn to blush.

"Did I say something wrong?" asked the doctor.

"No, not at all. It's just that nobody—well, except for my mother, nobody's ever told me that before. It's nice. Thank you."

"You're welcome, but it's the truth. So, have you decided

what you would like to eat?"

"Well, I've always wanted to try the classic Surf and Turf. But it's so expensive."

Dennis waved his arms dismissively. His warm expression put her at ease. "You can order whatever you like. It's on me."

What a gentleman! Eve was beginning to think that it didn't matter what Dennis may or may not be expecting in return. It had been far too long since any man had treated her this way.

The waiter returned and Dennis ordered Surf and Turf for Eve, and Fillet Steak, medium-rare, for himself. He poured two glasses of wine and pushed hers across the table.

"So," he said. "Tell me about yourself. Have you always wanted to be a nurse?"

She took a sip of wine. "Oh yes. My whole life, all I've wanted to do was help people. Nursing just seemed like the logical choice."

Dennis raised an eyebrow. "Oh? Why not a doctor?"

"Too much work. Besides, you doctors never really have the personal relationships we have with the patients. You come in, bark orders, and leave. We have to explain to the patients what's happening, and answer their questions." She felt her face grow hot. "Oh, I'm sorry. No offence."

"None taken." He winked at her. "Do you live alone?"

The question was so left-field that Eve recoiled, and choked on a sip of wine. She was about to answer that no, she didn't, but then she remembered. She burst into tears.

Dennis immediately shifted his chair around to sit next to her. He put his arm around her shoulders. "Hey. It's okay. What's wrong? I'm sorry."

"'s fine," blubbered Eve. "S-so sorry. You m-must think me a fool. I'm embarr-assing you."

"No, you're not," cooed Dennis, although truthfully, people

were beginning to stare. "Come now, tell me. Tell me all about it."

And so she did. She started with last night, and her fight with Aiden, and worked her way backwards. Before she knew it, she'd told him their entire history together, all the pain and suffering, all the way back to him catching her eye at some random pub ten years ago.

By the time she'd finished, she'd regained her composure somewhat. As she sniffed, their food arrived. The waiter saw the tears on her cheeks and gave an apologetic shrug as he placed their plates in front of them and backed away.

Dennis asked her if she wanted to leave.

"No," she said. "This is nice. Thank you for listening. Sorry for offloading on you like that." She picked up her lobster and broke it open with her hands. Then she realised she wasn't sure how to eat it, so she put it down again. Dennis just grinned at her.

She blushed. "But let's change the subject," she said. "Tell me about yourself."

"Well, I've always known I wanted to be a doctor," he began. He told her about medical school, and how for him, it was all about making a difference in people's lives. Many of the other students just wanted to pull girls, but that was never his thing. Besides, he confessed, he always had trouble talking to girls, and his fellow students would often pick on him because of it.

Eve listened attentively, nodding and patting his arm sympathetically. She let him talk. It seemed like the least she could do. But it felt as though he were holding back something, that his school years were more painful than he'd let on.

"Dessert?" he asked when they'd finished their food.

She pushed her plate away and shook her head. "Nuh-uh. That was wonderful, but I really couldn't eat another bite."

"As you wish, my lady," he said, and chuckled. Then he

called the waiter over. "May we have the bill, please?"

When Dennis dropped Eve off at home, he was again the perfect gentleman. He got out of his car, walked around to the passenger door, opened it, and helped her out of the car. Then he walked her to her front door.

Standing at the front door, Eve looked up at his face. At first, it seemed as though he was leaning in for a kiss, but then he pulled back.

"Well, that was fun," he said. "Thank you for joining me."

"Thanks for inviting me."

There was that almost-kiss again. Eve wasn't sure how she would've reacted if he *had* tried. It had only been a friendly dinner, after all. Still, it would've been nice to know that he wanted to.

She opened her mouth, about to invite him in for a cup of coffee, when he spoke again.

"I'd best be off. Are you going to be okay all alone?"

No, you dolt, she wanted to say. *I want you to come inside, to spend a couple more hours with me, at least. Then, see what happens.*

But she didn't say any of those things. All she said was, "Ja, thanks. I'll be fine."

He took her hand, and she thought he would at least kiss *that,* but he didn't. He just shook it and said, "Well, goodbye then. See you at work tomorrow."

Then he left.

Eve's heart fluttered as she watched the car drive out of sight. She opened her front door and stepped inside. The house was dark and empty. It was past eleven, and for a second she expected to hear Aiden's soft snoring coming from the bedroom, but all was silent. She walked into the bedroom, flicked on the light, and got ready for bed.

Twenty minutes later, she was fast asleep, visions of Doctor Dennis Wilson filling her dreams.

Gloria Gaynor's *"I Will Survive"* jolted her awake. Her cellphone screen glowing brightly on the bedside table. Picking it up, she saw two things: Aiden was calling, and it was three in the morning.

Instinctively, she answered the phone.

"Aiden, what's wrong?"

Aiden's angry voice, slurred from some kind of drug-induced stupor, shot back at her. "What's wrong, you stupid bitch, is that you went on a date tonight. A date! With that dork? Have you no shame?"

Eve let out an exasperated sigh. "Aiden, I have a right to spend some time with a friend. And how do you know? Are you stalking me?"

"Call it what you want. *I* have a right to know what my fucking girlfriend's doing when I'm not around."

"Aiden, are you high?" Eve was trembling now. "You know what, it doesn't matter. We're taking a break. I need a break. And I can't do this right now. We'll talk later. Bye."

Eve hung up, still trembling. She'd heard stories before of jilted ex-lovers going over the edge and doing stupid things. She really hoped Aiden wouldn't turn out to be one of those.

he phone rang again. Still Aiden. She rejected the call and switched off the phone.

She dropped it back onto her bedside table, buried her head in her pillow, and sobbed herself back to sleep.

Eve's alarm clock went off two and a half hours later. She woke up and discovered her head felt like someone was knocking her brain around with a sledgehammer. Her first thought was that she hadn't drunk that much last night. Two glasses of wine at the most. But then she remembered the phone call. She switched on her phone. Three more missed calls from Aiden. One voicemail. She dialled in and listened to it:

"Baby, I'm so sorry. I never meant to talk to you that way. Please call me back. You know, I've told you before that I believe in guardian angels. I believe there's been one looking out for us, and you have your own personal one too. I felt him last night. I nee—"

The message cut off. Aiden's thirty seconds were up. There were no more messages. He'd sounded pretty high, so Eve surmised that he must've fallen asleep after that.

She briefly considered calling him back, but she really still couldn't face talking to him. Besides, she needed to get to work. Maybe a bit later in the day, if he gave her some space, she might feel ready.

She arrived at work an hour later. Simone was waiting for her, and pounced the second she walked in the door.

"And? How was it? Did he? Did you? I want to hear *everything*. Spill it, sister!"

Eve chuckled and waved her away. "Nothing much to tell. Dennis was the perfect gentleman. We had a nice dinner, he dropped me off at home, and that was that."

"Dennis? Oh, we're on a first-name basis now, are we? Well, that just won't do. Tell me more, honey."

"Maybe later." Eve chuckled. "Right now, we need to get back to work."

Nothing much happened that day. The most exciting patient they had was a middle-aged lady who had called an ambulance to drive her to the hospital because she had a stomach ache. It turned out to be nothing more than mild indigestion.

Dennis attended on that case, while Eve assisted. He was the picture of professionalism; other than the occasional knowing look he shot her way, nobody would ever have guessed that they were any more than work colleagues.

Aiden tried to phone her at least five more times, and each time she rejected the call. She was getting angrier and angrier, and by the third time, she'd made up her mind that she would *not* be talking to him today.

Eventually, she got a smoke break, and decided to listen to her messages. She snuck out, trying not to let Simone see her. Her friend would still have a thousand questions about last night, and she wanted to be alone.

She sat down on the concrete bench, lit up a cigarette, and dialled her voicemail.

"You have four new messages.

"First message:

"Baby, it's Aiden. Did you get my message last night? I really need to talk to you. Please call me back.

"Next message:

"Eve, I'm sure you're swamped at work, but we need to talk. I wasn't joking about the guardian angel thing.

"Next message:

"Listen here, you stupid fucking bitch. If you don't call me back right now—"

Eve pressed 7 on her phone's keypad.

"Message deleted. Next Mess—"

She hung up. She couldn't hear any more.

Simone came outside and lit up a cigarette. She noticed the tears welling up in Eve's eyes.

"What's wrong, babe? Did Doctor Wilson say something?"

"No, it's not that," said Eve, and dried her eyes with a

tissue. "I don't want to talk about it."

Simone sat down next to her and patted her on the knee. "Well then, you don't have to. What are friends for, anyway? So, tell me more about last night."

Eve chuckled. "Last night was actually perfect. Just what I needed. He was the perfect gentleman, like I said. We just talked and talked. He told me all about his life, and I told him all about mine."

"*All* about yours?" Simone raised an eyebrow.

"You mean Aiden. Yes, he knows all about it."

"And that didn't scare him away? Girl, you've got a keeper."

Eve laughed heartily for the first time in days. She stood up and stubbed out her cigarette. "Well, I should really be getting back to work."

Another four missed calls and two voicemails later (which she didn't bother listening to), Eve arrived home, exhausted and livid with Aiden. How dare he presume to talk to her like that. It's not like he owned her. Not now, not ever.

She opened the door, expecting the house to be empty. Only it wasn't. The TV was on. She glanced over at the couch and saw Aiden sitting there.

"Aiden, what are you—"

But then she looked closer. His eyes were rolled back in his head, staring eerily at the ceiling. There was a needle sticking out of his left arm, and just above it, a brown rubber tube was wound tightly around his bicep.

Oh shit, oh shit, oh shit.

The words just kept repeating in her mind, over and over. I couldn't get a read on what else she might be thinking, she was so panicked.

She darted over to him and pressed her fingers against his neck. No pulse.

Now it was my turn to panic. What had I done? This woman was my charge, I was supposed to be keeping her safe. I'd really messed this one up, hadn't I?

Eve pressed her lips against Aiden's and breathed. His mouth was cold. His lips were purple. She pounded on his chest, screaming at him, calling him all sorts of names, begging him to wake up.

He never did.

Finally, Eve collapsed onto the floor. Tears streaming down her face, breathing heavily. The man she'd spent the past ten years with was gone.

As her breathing began to slow, she noticed a piece of paper lying on a coffee table, a pen resting beside it. She picked it up and began to read:

My dear Eve. These past ten years spent with you
have been the best years of my life. I'm sorry to have
disappointed you so. I'm also sorry that I kept myself a
key. I feel as though my guardian angel has failed me,
and yours has failed you. I can't live in a world where
you don't want me anymore. Goodbye.

It wasn't like Aiden to be so formal. By the time Eve had finished reading, she was sobbing bitterly. And if I could, I'd be sobbing right along with her.

An idea sparked in her mind.

Well then, Aiden, if you can't live without me, I can't live without you. How do you like that?

She rushed to the bedroom and flung open Aiden's cupboard. She opened the safe, hoping that he'd forgotten to take the revolver. *I* was hoping against hope that he hadn't forgotten.

But he had. Eve pulled it out and, with her hands shaking, opened her mouth and wrapped her lips around the barrel.

No, oh please, no! I screamed.

Goodbye Aiden.

Dennis' face briefly flashed through her mind. She felt the tiniest pang of regret and had time to wonder what he would think.

She pulled the trigger anyway.

Memoirs of a Guardian Angel

Part II

Graham Downs

Chapter Seven

Do you remember me saying that I wished we guardian angels got to see how our wards' stories ended up?

Well, I take it back. I don't remember my mortal life, but I'm convinced that losing Eve was the worst thing to have ever happened to me. It's certainly the worst thing that's ever happened to me as an angel.

When she pulled that trigger, I felt like I was being ripped apart inside. I didn't have time to dwell on it, though, because that hated spiral quickly engulfed my vision. I wondered what I could have done to save Eve, and then I wondered what my next assignment would be.

But when the spiral dissipated, I saw nothing but blackness. I blinked a few times and could make out, all around me, vaguely humanoid shapes, outlined in all blue. I was back in the World Beyond the Veil.

The black void again stretched out under my feet, and I felt alone.

"Hey, Adam!" John, my trainer, called me over from the other side of what can only be described as a plaza.

Struggling to once again adjust to the strange form of locomotion, I made my way over to him.

"It's good to see you, Adam," said John. "But I only wish it was under better circumstances."

"What do you mean?"

"I'm really sorry about Eve. We were watching on the training screen. But that's not the worst of it. I'm afraid you've been placed under suspension. No more assignments for you until you've stood before the Tribunal."

"The Tribunal?" I asked, incredulous. "What on Earth is

that?"

"Not Earth, my friend. Not Earth. They set the rules for us guardians. And you've been charged with negligence of a ward under your care."

"What? Negligence? What could I have done?"

"I don't know all the details. I'm guessing their argument is that you could've changed reality so the gun wasn't there. Maybe even done something earlier, so it never got to that in the first place."

I stared at John and blinked. "But John, I tried. I really tried. Do you think I *wanted* her to die? No matter how hard I focused, I couldn't will the gun out of that safe."

John put his ethereal hand on my shoulder. "I know, Adam. Don't worry, I'm with you. We'll work this out. I promise we will."

"So," I asked John, as we sat quietly in his office. "Tell me more about this 'Tribunal'."

"They set the rules, as I said. And they enforce them rigorously. If they think you let a mortal die due to negligence, you could be in for a lot of trouble."

I wrung my hands nervously, unable to believe what was happening. "W-what kind of trouble?"

"Best we not dwell on that now." John's voice was soft, sympathetic. "Their envoy could collect you for the trial at any moment. We need to figure something out. Let's start at the end and work backwards. What can you tell me about the gun?"

Remembering was difficult. It was all a haze. When I tried to recall those last moments before Eve pulled the trigger, all I felt was sadness and helplessness. I told John so.

John patted my shoulder. "It's understandable that you don't remember. And in this case, it's probably a good thing. I watched the playback, and I felt you willing Eve to not find that gun. The fact that you feel such regret now implies that you never meant for any of this to happen."

I was about to respond when we were interrupted by a knock on the door.

In walked a female angel. Here in The World Beyond, her body was an incorporeal, translucent blue, but still, I recognised that face. This was Liz, the one I'd seen on the screen during those first days of my training.

"You must be Adam." She grabbed my hand and shook it furiously. "Sorry to disturb, but I'm back on a bit of leave, and I heard about you. Being trained by John, eh? Well, I can tell you that John's the best. He taught me everything he knows. Welcome to the team."

John blushed. "You really think I'm the best?"

"Of course I do," said Liz. "Anyway, they say you tried to emulate me on the roof of a car; it looks like I have a fan! I'm pleased to meet you.""Liz, Adam. Adam, Liz," introduced John. "It's good to see you, Liz, but I'm afraid now's not a good time. Adam here's in a bit of a jam, and we don't have much time."

"Oh, really? What kind of jam?"

John was about to tell Liz something like "None of your business", but I put my hand up.

"It's okay, John. Everyone will know soon enough. A woman—the woman I was meant to be protecting—died on my last assignment, and now the Tribunal's charging me with negligence."

Liz's eyes opened wide. She took a step back and put her hand on her chest. "Negligence? Gee, that's bad. If you're found guilty, you'll probably never be allowed in the field again. If they want to be especially mean, you could even be banished from here altogether and sent to the other place."

John and I gulped in unison. My voice was a whisper when I

responded. "The... other place?"

Liz perked up. "Oh, but don't worry. I'm sure that won't happen to you. You seem like a good guy, and I'm sure it's just a huge misunderstanding."

She got up to leave. "Well, let me not keep you. I wish you the very best of luck, and I promise to keep you in my thoughts."

With that, she gave a flourish and scurried out the door.

John spent the next few hours grilling me about the events that happened during my assignment with Eve. From Aiden's drug problem, to the job offer, to Eve's dinner with Dennis, and to the eventual overdose and suicide.

John knew everything already, it seemed. He told me he'd watched the recording of my assignment so many times it was ingrained into his memory, and he wanted to make sure that my account matched up. I still couldn't remember much, but as he spoke, things slowly started coming back to me. Even so, my most vivid recollections were emotions. Mostly pain and helplessness, but occasionally glimmers of joy, particularly when Eve was spending time with her friend Simone, and of course during her meal with the good Doctor Wilson.

I asked John if he thought it was a good idea to let me see the recording, but he shook his head, saying that he didn't want my recollection to become polluted by the facts. Whatever that was supposed to mean. He said that if I physically saw myself in those moments, I might start thinking I felt things I hadn't really felt.

I had my doubts, but I let it go. John had trained countless guardians, after all, while I was barely out of training.

"John," I asked at length, "why exactly do you believe me?"

"What do you mean?" asked John.

"Well, you've seen the same things as the Tribunal, and they believe I'm guilty of negligence. Or at least, they think there's enough evidence to warrant suspicion. Yet, you don't seem to doubt me for a second. Why is that?"

"I've spent a lot of time with you, Adam. During your training, I could tell you really cared about these mortals. I watched both your assignments, and I saw how hard you worked for Rebecca. And it's plain to me now how deeply Eve's death affected you. I just don't think you would've let that happen if you hadn't done everything you possibly could to stop it."

I opened my mouth to respond, but he cut me off.

"Besides, I know what negligence looks like. I... one of my trainees let somebody die, long ago. He was brought before the Tribunal and found guilty. I knew he did it, and I stood by and watched as they did terrible things to him. *You*, my boy, were not negligent. And I will not see them do the same things to you."

A tear ran down my cheek. I wiped it away just as Liz burst through the door.

"John," she huffed. "Adam. I'm really sorry to disturb you, but there's something you both need to know."

"Go on," said John.

"Well, I tried to watch Adam's last assignment," she began. "I'm sorry. I shouldn't have done that. But I know you, John, and you wouldn't say he was innocent if you didn't believe it with everything you have."

She looked around conspiratorially before continuing. "Well, it's the strangest thing. When I pulled the assignment up on the monitor, all I saw was blackness. I knew something was there, but it was like I was being prevented from seeing it somehow."

"Interesting," said John. "Why do you think that was?"

"I don't know," said Liz. "Nothing like that's ever happened to me before."

There was another knock on the door, and a stern-faced

angel walked in. Standing at attention, he announced, "I come as an envoy for the Tribunal. They wish to speak with the guardian angel known as Adam."

John turned to Liz. "Well, it may be moot now. We're on. Go, see what you can find out." Then, turning to me, "It's time, my friend."

John and I walked side by side, following the envoy into the Tribunal chambers. After he'd escorted us in, the envoy left.

It really wasn't what I was expecting. The room was nothing but inky blackness. Above me, all around me, below me. John and I saw three glowing forms, hovering above us. Aside from that, we were alone.

"Speak only when spoken to," whispered John. "Address them as 'Sirs', and be confident."

A deep voice boomed from the middle form. "Adam, you are charged with negligence in the matter of the death of the mortal Eve Matthews. How do you plead?"

I swallowed hard, but remembering John's instructions, I composed myself and tried to speak as calmly as possible. "I am not guilty, Sirs. I did everything I could to prevent the death of my ward."

"Yes," cried John. "He's innocent!"

"Silence," said the voice. "That will do, for now."

"Let us continue," said a slightly higher pitched voice, coming from the second form. "When the accused arrived in the victim's world, where was he?"

A third voice responded. "He was on the roof of a car, and the victim was behind the steering wheel."

"Yes," interjected John excitedly. "That's right. And he stopped her from having an accident. How is that 'negligent'?"

The first voice came again with a force of thunder, shaking

the chambers and almost making me fall to my knees. "Enough! Need we remind Guardian Angel Trainer John that he is here at the pleasure of this court? He does not need to be here. One more outburst and he will be ejected."

John shrank back, and his voice broke as he answered. "Yes, Sirs. My apologies."

"Good," said the voice. "We shall proceed."

"Indeed," said the second voice, once again. "When the victim returned home, the accused allowed her to be swayed by the drug addict, Aiden Singer. Did he fail to notice this Aiden's manipulation of the victim, and foresee what might come?"

I gulped. I still didn't remember many specifics, but I had a recollection of averting my eyes, letting my sense of modesty cloud my judgement. I had to admit as much to the Tribunal, but also that the whole assignment was very much a haze in my mind.

"I see," said the third voice again. "So, the accused admits that he can't recall the details of the assignment. Did the outcome mean so little to him?"

"Sirs," I began, trying to speak as clearly as possible. "My trainer posits that it is *because* I care so much that I cannot remember. All I feel when I think of the whole ordeal is sadness and regret."

"The accused's level of remorse is not in question here," responded the second voice. "Although it may serve as a mitigating factor in his sentencing, should it come to that. What is in question is whether the accused, through his negligence, caused the death of the victim, Eve Matthews. Is that clear?"

"Y-yes, Sirs," I stammered.The trial went on that like for hours. The blackness of the room seemed to engulf me, as I sank deeper and deeper into it. I realised that they were right. With Rebecca, I actively participated in keeping her safe, from the time she was three years old, up until the point where I saved her from the razor-blade.

With Eve, there were so many times I could have intervened. But I did nothing. I could've done so many things. Why had none of them occurred to me at the time? Why could I not remember any of the specifics?

By the time the Tribunal had finished, I was prepared to shout at the top of my lungs, "Enough. Enough. I'm guilty. I don't deserve to be a guardian angel. Throw the book at me. Everything you have. Sentence me to the deepest, darkest pit of eternal damnation."

But I was too afraid. I didn't say any of those things.

"This court has heard enough," said the first voice. "We find that the accused, the guardian angel known as Adam, had ample opportunity to save the life of the victim, Eve Matthews. He did nothing. Therefore, he is henceforth forbidden from any further contact with the mortal world."

John and I gasped. He looked at me, sympathy pouring from his eyes.

"However," continued the first voice. "We have also seen enough evidence to show that the accused is remorseful of his crimes. It is this court's determination, therefore, that he be permitted to remain in this realm. That is all. We are adjourned."

With that, the three forms disappeared, leaving John and I standing alone in the darkness.

Chapter Eight

"And then I told him, 'That's what she said!'"

On the screen, a group of men in Boer War uniforms lounged around a table in a smoky bar, playing cards. The group roared with laughter, and I saw the joke teller's angel standing behind him, laughing right along with them.

Liz walked up behind me and put her hand on my shoulder. "I'm sorry about what happened with the Tribunal."

"Idiot," I said to the screen, not registering her presence. "Doesn't he understand how pointless this is?"

"Who? The man telling the joke?"

"No, his angel. We get sent out there to help protect people. But it makes no difference. That man could walk out of that bar and take a bullet to the head, and there'd be nothing his angel could do about it. Then he'd get hauled in front of the Tribunal and get found guilty of negligence."

"Adam, I need to tell you something," said Liz. "I've found out why I can't see your recording."

"It doesn't matter," I said, and waved her away.

Liz grabbed me and turned me around to face her. "Yes, it does. Adam, listen to me. I thought it was strange, because nothing like that's ever happened to me before, but then I remembered something John taught me when I first became an angel. He said nobody could take part in anything involving their own mortal lives."

"Ja, so?" I shrugged.

"So I pulled some strings, and got a friend of mine at archives to pull my file."

"Your *what*?"

"My file. All about my mortal life. We all have one, but

you're not supposed to ever read your own. Anyway, I pulled some strings and got hold of mine. And Adam, I think I was Eve Matthews."

I took a deep breath and told Liz to start at the beginning.

Apparently, our files don't contain our human names, but Liz said that she had shot herself when she was mortal, after seeing her drug addict boyfriend overdosed on heroin and reading his suicide note.

When she'd finished, I blinked at her. "Okay, so you're—were—Eve. That's quite a coincidence. I mean, what are the chances? I still don't see how it helps me."

"You're right, Adam, it is a coincidence. Too much of a coincidence. I don't think it's actually forbidden, but I've never heard of an angel's case having anything to do with the mortal life of a member of the same team. Think about it, there are billions of guardian angels out there, and millions of angel teams. Why assign you to a case involving an angel with the same trainer as you?"

I didn't have an answer for that one.

"Also," she said. "Maybe it has something to do with why you can't remember any specifics. Have you seen the recording?"

"No," I said. "But I think it's about time I did. Let's go find John."

John listened intently to Liz's story, rubbing his chin.

"Interesting," he said. "Yes, I suppose it would make sense. It's the only explanation I can think of, at any rate, for why you couldn't see the recording."

"John," I said. "Do you think now would be a good time to let me see it?"

"Well," replied John. "The trial is over, and you're technically not a guardian angel anymore."

"Thanks for putting it so bluntly." I felt tears well up all over again.

"Yes, well, sorry about that. I wish there was something more we could do, but there isn't. Anyway, as I was saying, I don't think there's any harm in it now. If you're sure you want to, that is."

I most definitely was sure I wanted to. More and more, I was buying into Liz's logic. Something was not right, and the answer would be in there somewhere.

"All right then," said John. "Let's call it up."

John called up the recording of the Eve Matthews assignment and pressed Play. I saw nothing but a blank screen.

"Are you sure it's playing?" I asked. "I see nothing."

"See?" said Liz. "That's what I was talking about. It's just nothing."

"I don't see anything either," said John. "Strange. Maybe it's just because you're here, Liz. Would you leave the room, please?"

Liz got up and walked out. When John and I were alone, he said, "Okay, let's try this again."

But the result was the same. Nothing but a blank screen.

"I was just watching this again before you arrived," said John. "I don't understand it. Maybe someone deleted it?"

"No, I don't think so," I said, getting excited. "I think it's because of me. I'll leave, and then you try again, okay?"

"I don't see how it could have anything to do with you." John scratched his head. "Angels watch their own recordings all the time, to hone their skills. There is absolutely no reason why you being here should affect it in any way."

"Just humour me, John."

John sighed. "All right, Adam. Please leave the room."

I went outside and found Liz standing there.

"And?" she asked.

"Still nothing. I told John to try again after I'd left."

"Do you really think—" was all Liz could get out before a voice came from inside.

"Incredible! Just incredible!"

As soon as I walked back in the room, the screen John was watching went black. Liz arrived a few seconds behind me.

John gawked at us, his mouth gaping open.

"So," he said, "we can't view the assignment with Liz here. And we're fairly certain she's a major player in the scenario. We can't view the assignment when you're here. So that can only mean—"

"That I'm a major player as well," I finished. "That's even more of a coincidence, but I'm still not sure that's not all it is."

"Oh, this is more than a coincidence," said John, waving his finger. "It may not be strictly against the rules to take part in an assignment involving a team member. But this... No angel can take part in one that directly affects his or her mortal life. This is absolutely forbidden. And it's probably why you struggle to remember it, too."

"What do you mean?" I asked.

"Adam, have you ever wondered why you can't remember details about when you were alive? I mean, you can remember things like Hitler or the Boer War, but you can't remember anything about your own life?"

I pressed my finger to my chin. "Well, now that you mention it, that is a bit strange."

"I can't remember if I told you this during training, boy, (I must've, or I wasn't doing my job properly) but there's a reason we angels can't remember anything about our mortal lives. We are, quite simply, forbidden to know. Which is also why we're forbidden from taking assignments involving those lives. We wouldn't be given those assignments. Ever. It just wouldn't happen."

Liz was wringing her hands, and her eyes were darting back and forth. "I-is it really that serious?"

"Oh yes," replied John. "You'd better hope whoever got you your file never tells, or you'll almost certainly find yourself in the other place."

"Don't worry," I said. "I'll never tell."

Liz' lip curled into a smirk. She asked, "Okay, but who could he be? Not Eve, we know that. How about that doctor she was dating? Or that friend of hers. Simone, was it?"

"Not Simone," I said. "Last I checked, I was a man."

"So?" said John. "Did I ever say we angels had to be the same gender as we were in life?"

I tried to picture myself as a woman. I shuddered.

John's demeanour changed. He was no longer a purely intellectual angel with a mystery to solve. He gripped both my shoulders and looked into my eyes, and once again he became the kind, concerned trainer-cum-father-figure.

"Adam," he said. "Listen to me very carefully. If we can prove you were given an assignment involving your mortal life, then the judgement can be overturned. You couldn't have done anything. You were powerless to interfere with your own mortal life. Do you understand what I'm saying to you?"

I gulped. Yes, I understood all too well.

"Oops," said Liz, interrupting. "I think my leave is over. I'm being called back."

As we looked at her, she was blinking in and out of existence. She looked a bit green, and I knew she was probably seeing the spiral. She had my sympathies. I knew what that felt like.

Just before she disappeared completely, she uttered one last word. "Bye."

After Liz had left, John got a concerned look on his face.

"Don't worry," I said. "She'll be fine. She was born to work in the field."

"Yes, the field," said John. "I hope that's where she's gone. I mean, I'm sure that's where she's gone."

"What do you mean?" I asked. "Do you think she's been found out?"

John swallowed hard. "I don't know. Best not dwell on it." He looked at me. "I think we need to take a look at your file."

"Okay, but John, even if this works, I don't know. I'm not really sure I want to go back out there. Maybe I'm not cut out for this business."

"Of course you are," snapped John. "I knew from the moment I laid eyes on you. Besides, you were chosen, and the choosers know what they're doing."

"Do they?" I asked. "I mean, how do you know they didn't make a mistake? If we're right, they made a mistake with my assignment."

"Oh, no, they didn't," said John matter-of-factly. "That was no mistake. If we're right, somebody did this on purpose. And I intend to find out why."

"All right," I said. "Then we need to get hold of my file. Couldn't you just pop down to Archives and retrieve it?"

"Not that simple, I'm afraid. As a trainer, I'm not really allowed to see my students' files. And unlike Liz, I don't have those kinds of connections. At least, not ones I'd risk on such dangerous business."

His eye's glazed over for a second, and I knew he was thinking about Liz again. I hoped she was going to be okay.

"What I *can* do," he went on, "is to see if we can't get

another audience with the Tribunal. They need to know of this possibility, so they can look into it."

"Do you think they'd listen, though? They might not even agree to see us. We have no proof, after all. We're just grasping at straws."

"You're right. An audience with all three might be too much to ask for at this stage. But I know Gabriel's clerk. He was the one who said your remorse might be a mitigating factor in your sentence. He might be prepared to see us."

"Gabriel?" I asked, bemused. I was finding it difficult to see the Tribunal as anything other than balls of light, much less think they might actually have names.

John grinned at me. "They're just angels, Adam. Albeit ancient angels. They put on a show in court, but that's more to intimidate people than anything else. I must admit, it's very effective. They even had me scared, standing there in their presence."

"Anyway," he continued, "I think Gabriel might be our best bet. I'll contact my connection, and ask if he'll see us. You go get some rest. It could take a while."

John was right: it did take a while. The Tribunal members were obviously very busy angels.

Eventually, the two of us found ourselves standing in the audience chamber of the angel known as Gabriel, one of the members of the Tribunal.

From his appearance, you would never have guessed that this was one of the angels responsible for keeping all law in this realm, but John assured me that he was.

Gabriel was shorter than I was, and even through the translucent blue outline that marked everyone here, I could see that he had a warm and kindly face.

He saw me staring, and chortled.

"Not what you were expecting, am I?" His voice sounded normal as well, nowhere near that boom that had come from the shapeless form during my trial.

"Well," he said, "we do have to keep up a certain appearance during our ceremonial duties, don't we?"

John stepped forward, interrupting.

"Your eminence," he said, "Thank you for agreeing to meet with us. Certain things have come to my attention which, if proven, could nullify your judgement against the angel Adam."

"Oh?" replied Gabriel. "What sort of things?"

"I believe," replied John, "that on his last assignment, Adam was (whether deliberately or not, I do not know) thrust into a situation where one of the mortals involved was... himself, while he was alive."

Gabriel took a step back and brought his fist to his mouth. His eyes went wide. Once he'd composed himself, he asked, "And by what logic do you come to this conclusion?"

I looked at John. I didn't think he would betray Liz; even though Gabriel respected him enough to agree to this audience, he was still a member of the Tribunal, and I knew Liz would be in a lot of trouble if he found out how she'd come to her conclusion.

John was silent for a moment, and when he responded, he did so slowly, choosing each word carefully. "Well, Sir, I first became suspicious when I tried to show him the recording of his assignment, after the trial."

Gabriel stroked his chin. "Hmm, that's quite irregular, but I suppose it couldn't do any harm, since the trial was concluded."

"That's just it," said John. "When Adam was in the room, neither of us could view the recording. We just saw darkness. I thought perhaps someone had tampered with it in some way, so I asked him to leave. After that, I could view it again."

Gabriel turned to me. "Is this true?"

"Yes, Sir," I answered. "I swear to you, I still have no idea what's on that recording. As you know from my trial, I also don't remember much of the assignment itself. John said that was unusual, and he now believes my lack of memory might be the same reason I was unable to view the recording."

Gabriel stroked his chin again. "I must admit, I found that curious during the trial as well. With this new information, it's even more so." He turned to John. "You may be right, but I'd caution against jumping to conclusions. There are other things that could explain why Adam is unable to view the recording or recall details of the assignment. Thank you for bringing this matter to my attention. I will look into it, and get back to you."

Sensing that our meeting was at an end, I turned to leave, but John spoke up once more.

"One more thing, your eminence. One of my protégés, the angel known as Liz, has disappeared. You wouldn't happen to know where she is, by any chance?"

"As far as I know," answered Gabriel, "she is on assignment. Now, if that will be all, I said I would look into your concerns."

John shrugged, and he and I left his office.

Graham Downs

Chapter Nine

"Why'd you ask him about Liz?" I asked John as we sat in his office. He'd materialised a desk and a chair, to make us feel more comfortable after the emptiness that was Gabriel's chambers.

"Take a look at this." John turned and faced a flat screen that suddenly appeared on his wall.

"I don't see anything."

"That's my point," said John. "I can't find Liz anywhere. As her trainer, I should be able to track down any member of my team at any time. Liz is nowhere to be found."

"What do you think happened to her?"

John's brow furrowed. "I hate to think it, but maybe she was discovered, digging into her file. If so, they're holding her somewhere, questioning her."

"If that's true," I asked, "does that mean that Gabriel lied?"

John shook his head. "I don't think so. He has no reason to. He said as far as he knew, she was on assignment. If she isn't, he doesn't know where she is."

I shrugged. "Yes, I suppose you're right. We'll just have to wait and see."

Not long after that conversation, I was walking around The Void (which is what I'd taken to calling that inky blackness with no sky or ground). As usual, other angels were walking around me, all going about their business. I assumed some of them must've been guardian angels like me, but others seemed to be busying themselves with various things.

Then, in the distance, I noticed an angel that didn't look anything like the others. Where most of them were a translucent blue, this one was characterised by a bright red outline. I found this odd, but nobody else seemed to pay him any attention.

As I got closer, I noticed the scowl on his face, and that he had small black protrusions above his eyes; I could only describe them as "horns".

Curious why he was so different from the others, I waved, and called out to him. "Excuse me."

He turned to stare at me but didn't respond. Then, in a blink, he was gone.

I asked John about it, the next time I saw him.

"A red angel, you say?" He stroked his chin and stared into space. "No. No, I don't believe I've ever seen one of those. We're all blue here. I'd be very surprised to see a red angel."

"Well, nobody else was," I replied. "Nobody else paid him any mind."

John slapped me on the back. "I honestly think you're imagining things," he said. "If I saw a red angel, I'd be staring with my mouth hanging open, I can assure you. It must be all the stress. Adam, my friend, I think we need to do something to take your mind off all this."

But that wasn't to be; that day we were once again summoned to an audience with Gabriel.

As we stood before him, the angel cleared his throat.

"I have called the two of you back today, because I have information to share, and I think it's important that you are both aware of it."

John and I stared at him expectantly.

When Gabriel didn't elaborate, John broke the silence. "Yes, Sir. What is it?"

"Well," answered Gabriel, "I was attempting to retrieve Adam here's file from Archives so that I could see if there was any truth to your theory."

There was another pause. It seemed to go on forever before I spoke up. "Well, what did you find?"

"Patience, young angel." Gabriel looked at me like an angry parent would look at a child. "In answer to your question, I didn't find anything."

John let out an exasperated groan. "So everything's in order, then? Adam's assignment didn't have anything to do with his mortal life?"

"I did not say that, Angel John. I said I found nothing. Which is to say, Adam's file appears to have gone missing."

Our jaws dropped open.

"What do you mean, 'missing'?" fumed John. "Like, someone misplaced it?"

Gabriel put up his hand. "I'd suggest you remember who you're talking to, my friend. And the privilege you've been afforded here today."

John seemed to shrink several centimetres. "Yes, Sir. Sorry, Sir."

"Good. Now then, I do not think it was simply misplaced. Access to our Archives is closely guarded. Besides, for it to have been misplaced, somebody must have been looking at it. That, in itself, would be cause for suspicion. No, I believe it was stolen."

I was flabbergasted. "Well then, that settles it, surely. Whoever stole my file must be trying to cover something up. That I was, intentionally or not, sent on an assignment that directly affected my human life. So I couldn't be held responsible for anything that happened on that assignment, right? I'm cleared. I can go out in the field again."

Gabriel held up his hand. "Not so fast, young one. We don't know anything of the sort. For all we do know, one of the two of you stole your file."

I smacked my forehead. "Now why on Earth..."

"This isn't Earth," interrupted Gabriel. "And there's something else." He turned to John. "Your protégé, Liz. It has come to my attention that she has been apprehended, and will be appearing before our Tribunal tomorrow. She stands accused of tampering with, or arranging the tampering of, her own file. If she could be capable of that, perhaps she did the same to Adam's."

I glanced at John, hoping he wouldn't give anything up. He didn't. He just gasped incredulously. "But this is ridiculous. I've known Liz for a long time. She would never do anything like what you're suggesting."

"That may or may not be. We will find out in due time. In the meantime, I am not prepared to reconsider Adam's matter. Consider yourselves lucky I do not add the same charge to you. I may still do that."

John and I walked out of Gabriel's chambers, crestfallen.

"Could it get any worse?" I asked.

"It might," said John, "depending on what Liz tells them. She did what she did to help us. I hope she doesn't pay dearly for it."

"Yes," I replied, "but if she tells them everything, she probably will. But if she denies it, and they later found out she lied, it could be much worse, right?"

"Right. I suppose we'll just have to wait and see what happens tomorrow."

"Do you think they'll let us watch?" I asked.

John frowned deeply. "I shouldn't think so. As you remember, the Tribunal sessions are normally closed affairs. And unless Liz has said anything to make them think otherwise, this case has nothing to do with us."

His words weren't yet cold, and we were only a short walk away from Gabriel, when an angel came running up to us.

"Angels Adam and John," he announced. "By order of the Tribunal, your presence is requested at the trial of Guardian Angel Liz tomorrow. Please report to the Tribunal at the allotted time."

Graham Downs

Chapter Ten

The three of us stood together, watching the shimmering balls of light that were the Tribunal. John was in the centre, and he glanced first at me, then at Liz, before grabbing each of our hands. We were going to present a united front.

"Guardian Angel Liz," a voice boomed. "You have been charged with obtaining access to documentation about your earthly existence. What have you to say in your defence?"

Liz swallowed hard. "Sirs, I do not deny this."

John and I gasped. What was she doing?

"However," she went on, "I did what I did to prove Guardian Angel Adam's innocence. To prove that he was given an assignment that he could not possibly complete."

"Yes," boomed the voice. "We are aware of your intentions. That is why we have summoned Angels John and Adam here today as well."

"Then you know what I discovered, as well." Liz was trying to be brave, but she couldn't stop her voice from wavering.

"That is irrelevant. You violated the most sacred of our codes. Your punishment should be severe."

I suddenly remembered something, so I exhaled deeply and stepped forward. "Wise angels of the Tribunal, there is something that I believe should be brought to your attention. I saw a red angel."

The Tribunal was silent for a few moments. Eventually, one of them spoke: "That is a serious claim, angel Adam. Is there anyone who can verify it?"

"No," I admitted. "I saw him in a crowd, but I think I was the only one. Nobody else showed any sign that they did too."

"It's been a long time since anybody's seen a red angel," said the voice. "If there is one, it would be a grim matter indeed. We shall have to look into it. I warn you, though, the consequences will be dire if you are being dishonest with this Tribunal."

I opened my mouth to respond but was interrupted by a terrible grating noise filling the chamber. It seemed to be coming from everywhere around us, as well as inside my very being. It took a while to realise that the noise was evil cackling.

"Fools!"

Then, there was a blinding red light, hanging in the air in the centre of the chamber. It slowly descended onto the space where we were standing, and the three of us backed away to allow it room.

As it landed on the ground, it burst. We raised our arms against the glare, and when we lowered them again, the red angel stood before us. He was tall and muscular, less translucent than we were, and coloured a deep blood red. A permanent sneer was etched into his face, and completely opaque black horns sprouted from his head.

The chamber was completely silent, as he turned his face away from us and towards the three glowing balls of the tribunal.

"I cannot take your idiocy any longer," he said, his voice a metallic grating sound. "I stole Adam's file."

The three of us gasped, while the Tribunal rumbled. The great angels did not respond, however, as the red angel went on. "I also arranged for him to be assigned to Eve Matthews. I can't believe how easy it was."

The angel chuckled again, and this time the Tribunal members responded.

"Enough!"

It was Gabriel's voice, and as he spoke, another flash of light blinded us. When it dissipated, the red angel was surrounded by a cage of thick iron bars. He gripped the bars and shook violently, but they didn't budge.

"It is you who are foolish, Red Devil," said Gabriel. "What you have done shows the worst disdain for our purpose, our very existence. Allowing guardian angels to be involved in their own earthly lives is incredibly dangerous."

"There was no danger," spat back the devil. "Your rules are meaningless. Just because you've followed them since Creation itself, doesn't mean they're right. Think of all the good that could be done if we'd just allow—"

"Think of all the harm." Gabriel's voice was like an explosion, silencing the red devil and everyone else in the chamber. "This Tribunal will hear no more from you. You will remain behind those bars until we can decide what to do with you."

John opened his mouth to speak, "Um, Your Magnificence. Does this mean...?"

"It means nothing, Guardian Angel John. The three of you will return to your existence and await further instruction. We are adjourned."

"What was that?" I asked. We were all seated in John's office, unsure how to process what we'd just witnessed.

Liz spoke up. "I've heard of it happening before. An angel with such hatred for our ways, that they turn red. Such an angel will stop at nothing to destroy everything we hold dear, turn our rules upside down for their own nefarious ends. I'd always thought it was just a myth, though."

John shook his head. "It's not. I've seen it. The last time it happened, all of humanity changed forever. But it's been a long time, probably tens of thousands of human-years. It's difficult to say how long, exactly; as you know, time is very different in The

World Beyond The Veil. I'm sorry I lied to you, Adam. I just didn't want to believe it."

I waved the issue away. It didn't matter now.

"But what about Adam?" Liz asked John. "Do you think he might be allowed in the field again?"

"I don't know," replied John. "It's possible. We'll just have to wait and see what the Tribunal decides."

I stared at my feet. "Do I really *want* to, though? The last assignment I went on ended catastrophically. I'm not sure that responsibility's for me."

"Nonsense," said Liz. "You *know* why that assignment turned out the way it did. I'm convinced you were Aiden. And I was Eve. That's the point. This is exactly why such things aren't allowed."

I shrugged. "Whatever. I'm more worried about you, Liz. Whatever happened, you still broke the rules by reading your file. That hasn't changed."

Liz pursed her lips. "Yes, well, like John said, we'll just have to wait and see."

We seemed to be doing a lot of "waiting and seeing" lately. I wished there something I could actively *do*.

Sometime later, I was watching the screen alone in the training room. A man was pointing a gun at a woman's head, and I could feel the terror in her guardian angel as he knew he was powerless to stop it.

Liz walked up beside me, and I started slightly when I saw her.

"Look at that, Liz. Why do people put themselves through stuff like that? Why do we angels put ourselves through stuff like that?"

She moved closer. "I don't know why people do what they do, Adam. I guess they're weak and myopic, and can't see the damage they're doing to their lives. That's why we do what we do. If we can make a difference to just one life, save just one soul, isn't it worth it?"

"Maybe," I replied. "But Liz, I'm just not sure I'm cut out for it. I can't explain what went through my head when Eve... when *you* killed yourself. I'd never felt so helpless, so alone." Liz opened her mouth to speak, but I cut her short. "Yes, I know that wasn't my fault, that there was nothing I could have done. I should never have been put in that situation."

I returned my gaze to the screen. The gun popped. The woman screamed. The man with the gun chuckled evilly. The angel fell to his knees and wailed at the futility of it all. Then he disappeared.

"See, Liz," I went on, "the point is that *I* was in that situation. I've been where this poor angel is now. He'll probably go on to his next assignment. But I'm not sure I can do that."

Liz put her hand on my shoulder. "You might not have to, you know. But one thing I'm sure of, Adam. If you're cleared to go back, you won't be sent anywhere you're not ready to be sent."

No sooner had Liz finished speaking than the Tribunal emissary appeared. It was surreal. One moment, it was Liz and I talking. The next, there he was, standing between us.

"Urgent news from the Tribunal," the emissary bellowed. "It has been decided that, due to extenuating circumstances, the judgements against Guardian Angel Adam and Guardian Angel Liz, have been revoked. They are free to resume assignments in the field." Then, he disappeared.

Liz and I stared at each other with wide eyes. "What now?" I asked.

She shrugged. "I guess now things can get back to normal. We should be returned to active du—"

Liz winked out of existence. It was unsettling, to say the least—first the emissary, and now Liz.

I was left sitting alone, staring at the blank screen. I sat there for a moment before John came rushing in.

"Did you hear the news? You and Liz are returning to active duty."

"Yes," I replied. "Liz has just left."

"Well, don't just stand there. Let's take a look." John turned on the screen, and there she was, sitting in her armchair on the roof of a car, looking as happy as could be.

"Why are you still here?" asked John.

"I'm not sure. Liz said I'd probably be called when I was ready. So that must be it. I don't think I'll ever be ready. I don't think I want to go back."

"What do you mean?"

"Just what I said. What good can we do, John? I mean, really? We try to keep these humans out of harm's way, but the result's the same in the end."

John smacked me on the back of my head. I didn't know we angels were capable of feeling physical pain until that moment.

"Don't be an idiot," he snapped. "I trained you better than that. You should know by now that everything happens for a reason. Even if we don't see the difference we make in people's lives. We *do* make a difference. Some good always comes from what we do."

"Not to the people we help." I glared at him.

"Maybe. Maybe not. But that's irrelevant. Someone else could be affected by what our wards go through. And *their* lives could be better for it. That's not for us to judge."

I fell silent for a moment, considering. I'd never thought of it that way before. When I was assigned to Eve, although I should never have been, she had other people in her life. Who am I to say that those people's lives didn't turn out better because of what happened to her? Well, maybe not *better*, but certainly different.

I let out a long, slow breath. "Okay, John. Maybe you're right. Maybe I need to get back out there. But it's moot anyway, isn't it? None of us gets to decide when we're ready. And obviously, I'm not. Why am I still here?"

As soon as I said that, I felt that familiar wooziness. I tried to stand but I wobbled on my feet. The pinwheel was in front of my eyes again. Turning, turning, turning. I was going back. But was I ready?

I didn't have time to think about it anymore. It was happening. The pinwheel was reversing, and the scene was changing. As it cleared, I saw a man kneeling. A woman sat in front of him. She was moaning, and she had a fist-full of his hair. His head was pressed between her legs, as a pair of pants lay pooled around her feet.

I groaned. *Why does everything humans do have to be about sex?*

Graham Downs

Memoirs of a Guardian Angel

Part III

Graham Downs

Chapter Eleven

"Okay, okay, enough," the woman heaved. "Please, Sam. No more. You're going to give me a heart attack!"

She giggled as Sam rose to his feet, leaving her bottom half fully exposed. She left her legs spread wide, which left nothing to my imagination. I blushed and looked away, but then remembered how my modesty had gotten me into trouble with the whole Eve situation. I wasn't sure yet who I was supposed to be guarding, so I kept my attention on both of them.

"I'm going to make a cup of coffee, and then it's off to work," Sam said. "Can I make you one?"

"No thanks, babes." The woman brushed Sam's shoulder. "I'm going to surf the web for a bit, and then I'll probably get an early night."

I glanced at the clock on the wall. It was almost seven in the evening.

Sam walked into the kitchen, and I was pulled after him. So at least that settled that.

In the kitchen, he filled the kettle and switched it on, before a ringing sound came from his pocket. This was the first I'd noticed his attire: a white button-up shirt, thin black tie, jacket and trousers. He hadn't even removed his jacket while he was "servicing" the woman.

Sam pulled the phone out of his pocket and answered it.

"Hey, Alex!" He paced around the kitchen, then took a quick peek through the doorway at the empty chair where the woman had been sitting. He lowered his voice slightly. "Yip. Sure. Sorry, just got caught up with something with Audrey." He chuckled. "Ja, that kind of something. You know me so well. Okay, I'll meet you at the pub in twenty. See you later."

103

He hung up the phone and shoved it back in his pocket. Cursing under his breath, he opened the front door and shouted "Bye, babe!" before walking out and slamming it behind him.

The pub was a smoky affair. Sam parked his ancient Mazda CX-5 on the street and headed inside.

It was dimly lit, and full of men with long beards in tank-tops, their tattooed arms as thick as most people's thighs. A man with a flat cap and a grey beard stood behind the bar with a grimy cloth over his shoulder.

Well-dressed, clean-shaven Sam looked out of place, but he didn't act it. He walked into the place with an air of confidence and scanned the room. Seated at a table in the corner were a man in a white muscle top and a black crew-cut, and a women with long black hair. From what I saw of the crowd, she might have the only woman in the bar, but she too carried herself with confidence. As if she belonged.

The man spotted Sam and waved him over.

"Fuckin' A, bru!" he said as Sam approached. "Geez, you made it, hey? I almost thought you wouldn't."

Sam flashed an exasperated smile. "Hi, Alex. What's going on?"

"Sit, man, sit. Take a load off." Alex waved a waiter over and ordered a beer-battered hake and chips. Sam sat.

Alex lowered his voice to a dramatic whisper, which I could tell Sam just thought was ridiculous.

"This is Joanna," he said, nodding towards the woman. "Jo for short," he added, just as Joanna was extending her hand to shake.

"Pleased to meet you," said Sam.

The woman raised her eyebrows. "Likewise."

"This is the oke I was telling you about, Jo. Anything that needs doing, our old pal Sam can do. Gua-ran-teed."

"Alex, dear," Joanna crooned, "would you mind going to the bar and getting me a glass of wine? Oh, and..." she looked at Sam questioningly.

"Beer," said Sam.

"And a beer for Sam," finished Joanna.

"But Jo, we just ordered food. Besides, we can grab a waiter —" He stopped as Joanna intensified her gaze.

"Right. Okay, I'll be right back."

"That's no problem. Take your time."

When Alex had gone, Joanna reached into her handbag and took out a pack of ultra-thin cigarettes in a rose-coloured box. She removed one and placed it between her lips. Sam stuck his hand in his pocket, produced a lighter, and lit it for her. *A gentleman should always keep a lighter in his pocket.* He smiled at the thought.

"Thank you," she said, before replacing the cigarettes in her bag and retrieving a manila folder. She placed the folder on the table. "Alex says you solve problems." She pointed to the folder. "He's a problem. Solve him."

Sam opened it. Inside was a pile of papers, on the top of which was a photograph of a man with a round face and a handlebar moustache.

"Who's he?"

"Everything you need to know is in those papers," replied Joanna. She reached a final time into her handbag and came out with a bulging envelope. This too, she placed on the table. "Twenty thousand. Call it a show of good faith. There'll be another twenty when my problem is solved."

She walked away just as Alex returned with the drinks.

"Yoh, she's a strange one, hey?" said Alex, sitting down. "Fine piece, though, you have to admit."

Sam agreed, then reached for the envelope on the table.

Alex got to it first. Scooping it up and opening it, he said, "Twenty grand, hey? This lady must really be desperate. What you gonna do?"

"My job." He snatched the envelope out of Alex's hands, tucked the folder under his arm, and stormed out the door.

What a dick, thought Sam as he exited the pub. *Why I put up with him I'll never know. Oh, right, because he brings me work.*

Sam stepped off the curb and onto the street, just as a yellow hatchback came careering down on a collision course. My heart leapt into my throat and, without thinking, I grabbed him by the scruff of his neck. He stumbled backwards and ended up sitting on his bottom on the pavement.

"Fuck," he muttered before standing up and patting dust off his pants. "How could I be so clumsy?"

Sam may not have known the danger he was in, but my chest puffed at a job well done. I didn't agree with what my ward did for a living, but it was still my responsibility to keep him alive. Besides, maybe something could be done to change his ways.

"Honey, I'm home!" Sam chuckled at his joke as he walked through the front door. Audrey, seated on the couch, didn't seem amused.

"Where have you been?" she asked irritably. "I've been trying to call. Why is your phone off?"

"It isn't." Sam reached into his pocket and pulled out his phone. He tried to unlock it, but the screen stayed off. "Crap," he said. "Battery's dead. I'm sorry, babe. I've been in a meeting."

Audrey glanced at the folder under his arm, and the bulge coming from his jacket, caused by the wad of cash in his pocket. She took a deep breath and folded her arms.

"The hospital called. It's your mother. She had an accident, and they tried to get hold of you. When they couldn't, they started phoning random numbers out of her contacts, and got to me."

Sam's mouth hung open. "Wait, what? How? What happened?"

"I don't know. I'm not family, so they wouldn't give me any details. If you'd bothered to charge your phone..."

Sam dropped the folder onto the table. It fell open, revealing the photograph of the man he'd just been hired to eliminate. He didn't care. He grabbed Audrey's arm and dragged her out of the house. "Let's go. What hospital's she in?"

Graham Downs

Chapter Twelve

An old woman lay in a bed in the corner of the ward. Of the six beds in the ward, two were occupied: the woman, and a young lady on a drip opposite her.

Sam and Audrey entered, and the woman's face lit up. "Sam, my boy. My handsome boy."

Sam approached the bed and gave his mother a hug. "Hi, ma," he said. "What happened to you?"

His mother was about to answer when she spotted Audrey. Instantly, her face contorted into a scowl.

"Hi, Ma Becky," said Audrey, and leaned in for a kiss. Becky turned her face, and let Audrey kiss her on the cheek instead.

"What's she doing here?" asked Becky.

"Oh, ma, please let's not get into that now," returned Sam. "Audrey told me you were in the hospital, and I came as soon as I could. Now, what happened?"

Becky's face softened. "It's nothing, my boy. I was reaching for the coffee on the top shelf, and I slipped and fell. That's all."

"Your mother's downplaying the seriousness of her situation."

Sam and Audrey turned to see a tall, slim man in a white lab-coat enter the room.

"I'm Doctor Deetleefs." He shook Sam's hand. "And your mother had a bad fall and broke her hip. She's in a lot of pain, and on morphine." Audrey glanced at the intravenous needle in Becky's wrist. "They'll be wheeling her into surgery within the next hour or so."

Sam gasped. "Ma, is this true? Why didn't you tell me?"

"Because I didn't want you to worry," she snapped back, then shot an accusatory glance at Doctor Deetleefs. "And I didn't want you to take me away from my *home*."

"Oh, ma." Sam ran his hand through his hair. "You know I'll always worry about you. I love you. But let's not talk about this now." He lifted his mother's hand—the one without the needle—and kissed it. "You just get better, okay?"

Becky beamed up at her son, then glanced at Audrey. It was clear she still didn't appreciate Sam's choice in women, but even so, her scowl was... softer, somehow.

As we exited the room, the strangest thing happened. Becky stared directly at me. It was as if she could see me, even though I knew that was impossible. It might have been a coincidence, but I could swear I saw recognition flicker in those eyes.

Sam and Audrey sat on the thinly upholstered wooden chairs in the hospital's cold waiting room.

"Do you think she'll be all right?" asked Sam.

Audrey brushed his cheek and said, "I'm sure she will, babe. She'll be back to her old, annoying self in no time."

"Don't joke," Sam said with a smirk. "I'm really worried about her."

Audrey leaned in and kissed him on the cheek. "I love you, you know that? Even though your mother can be infuriating at times."

Before Sam could respond, Doctor Deetleefs came walking up to them, wearing surgical scrubs. A mask hung around his neck.

"Your mother's going to be fine," he said. "The operation was a success. It looks like the pins are going to hold."

Sam stood up. "Can we see her?"

"Yes, but she's sleeping. It'll be a few hours before she wakes up. And we're going to need to keep her here overnight for observation. You two should probably go home."

Audrey squeezed Sam's hand. "Come, babe. The doctor's right. Let's go get some sleep."

"One more thing," said the doctor. "When she goes home, she's not going to be able to be alone for a while. At least a couple weeks. She'll need someone to help her get around until she's back on her feet."

"That's okay," said Sam. "She can stay with us. Can't she, babe?"

Audrey smiled wanly, but I saw the dread in her eyes. I knew Sam saw it, too. "Sure, babes. Of course she can."

"It's after midnight, babes." Audrey yawned as they opened the front door and walked into their lounge. "Let's get some sleep."

Sam sat down on the couch. "You go ahead, angel. I've got this file to go through tonight. Work waits for no man."

Audrey sighed. "Okay, but not too late, okay?" She kissed him on the forehead. "Goodnight."

Sam was glad Audrey didn't know what he really did. At least, she never mentioned it. She'd never asked him what he did for a living, and he'd never given her any details. She knew he carried a gun, but he didn't think she knew what he did with it.

After Audrey left, Sam pulled his laptop out of the bag, set it on the coffee table, and booted it up. While he was waiting, he opened the file.

The photo was a middle-aged balding man with a black moustache. He looked Indian. Sam flipped up the photo and read the file behind it. The subject's name was Pravesh Moonsamy. He was the CEO of a multi-national oil conglomerate, headquartered here in the city. He had a wife and three children. There wasn't much more in the file.

Sam stroked his chin, then entered Moonsamy's name into Google. There wasn't much there, either. The company had just signed a merger agreement with a smaller company in The States. There were some reports of the astronomical salaries earned by company executives, while the workers earned so little. The usual stuff.

What's so special about this guy? thought Sam as he picked up the phone and started dialling.

A few seconds later, Alex's sleepy voice came on the other end of the line.

"Sam? Fuck, bru, do you know what time it is? What's wrong?"

Sam glanced at his watch. "Ja, sorry, Alex. I'm just doing some research on this latest assignment. What do you know about Joanna?"

"What? Sheesh, man, not much, hey. Hey, can we talk about this in the morning? I really want to get some sleep, here."

Sam snorted when he heard a woman's voice in the background. "Alex?" She stifled a yawn. "Who's that? Is everything okay?"

"No problem, boet," said Sam into the phone. "Catch up tomorrow. Bye."

Oh well, not going to get much work done tonight. He chucked the phone on the couch next to him, closed his laptop, and sat back, lacing his fingers behind his head. His thoughts turned to his mother.

Or more specifically, to his mother's relationship with Audrey. He loved his mother, but he loved his girlfriend, too. He'd been thinking of asking Audrey to marry him for a while now. The only thing stopping him thus far had been his mother's feelings towards his (hopefully) fiancée to be. He couldn't understand why his mother couldn't see what he saw in Audrey. The funny, witty, smart Audrey. The Audrey who turned men's heads wherever they went, but always went home with him. Sure, they had their fights from time to time. What couple didn't? But they always found a way to sort it out.

And now Ma Becky would be coming to stay with them. Sam chuckled to himself as he wondered if both of the women in his life would make it out alive.

Then there was his job. Who was he kidding? Of course Audrey suspected what he did, but she had the good sense to keep her nose out of his business. Killing people for a living had a way of earning you enemies, and Sam shuddered to think about the danger Audrey would be putting herself in if she got more involved.

His mother, though, wasn't so discreet. She knew exactly what Sam got up to after dark. She'd never turn him in to the police or anything, but she made her feelings quite clear on the matter: find a normal job, one that didn't involve hurting people for a living, or be disinherited.

Not that his mother had loads of money, anyway. But still....

With these thoughts swimming in his head, Sam succumbed to sleep.

At four in the morning, Sam was woken by the shrill ring of his cellphone. Sleepily, he reached for it on the coffee table. He'd been sleeping sitting up for around two hours, and he felt it in his neck.

Without checking who was calling, he picked it up.

"Hello?"

"Hi, Mister Anderson? It's Sister Janine here from Saint Joseph's. It's about your mother. She's taken a turn for the worse. Doctor Deetleefs said I should give you a call. We think you need to come."

Sam's eyes went wide, and he almost dropped the phone. "What? Why? What happened?"

"I really don't think it's appropriate to tell you any more over the phone, sir. Please just come."

With that, she hung up.

Sam wasted no time. He leapt to his feet and stormed into the bedroom. Audrey was just waking up. "Babe, where have you been? Did you sleep on the couch?"

"No time," Sam shot back. "You need to get up, get dressed." He opened the cupboard and started throwing her clothes onto the bed. "We need to go. Now. Hospital called. Mom's in trouble."

Audrey propped herself up on her arms. "Oh, babe, I'm so sorry. Is she...?"

"I don't know. They wouldn't tell me. Just hurry, will you? I'll go start the car."

Sam stormed out of the house, found the car parked on the street, and pulled the handle. The door didn't open.

Shit, he said under his breath. *Keys.*

He raced back inside, almost bowling Audrey over, as she stood in the doorway putting on her shoes.

"Babe, please just *slow down*!"

At the hospital, Sam and Audrey didn't bother stopping at Reception. They raced into Becky's ward, where she lay with tubes sticking out of her nose and electrical cables stuck to her chest. Dr Deetleefs was there, standing over her.

He turned when they entered the room.

"Mister Anderson, thank you for coming."

"I came as quickly as I could," said Sam, huffing and puffing. "What happened? Is she...?"

Memoirs of a Guardian Angel

"No," replied the doctor. "Your mother went into cardiac arrest about an hour ago. We were able to stabilise her, and she should be fine. It does mean that we'll have to keep her under observation a few more days, though."

"But Sister Janine gave me the impression—"

Doctor Deetleefs held up his hand. "Sister Janine is prone to overstating things from time to time. Don't get me wrong: cardiac arrest is serious. And it means she'll have to make some lifestyle adjustments when she does go home. But right now, she's not dying."

"Is she awake?" asked Audrey.

"No. She's sleeping. But it's just sleep." said the doctor, "I have rounds to do, but you can stay as long as you like. Have Sister Janine page me if you need me."

With that, he made his exit.

"The doctor's wrong, you know." It was Becky. Her eyes were open but glassy, and she spoke in a soft voice.

"What do you mean, Ma?" asked Sam. "How much did you hear?"

"Everything, son." Ma Becky coughed into her fist. "And I tell you, he's wrong. I'm dying, Sam. I don't know how long. Maybe hours. Maybe days. But I feel it in my soul."

Sam ran to her bedside and took her hand in his. He squeezed it as he spoke. "Don't be ridiculous, mother. You won't be here long, and then you can come stay with us." He glanced at Audrey. She just shrugged. "You'll see. The doctor says you're going to be all right."

I could see that Sam didn't really believe it. His heart was racing at a mile a minute, and panic had him in an icy, vice-like grip.

Becky beckoned him closer and lowered her voice. "Now you listen to me. I don't have much time left, but I will *not* leave this Earth knowing that you kill people for a living. And you," she glared at Audrey. "We've never seen eye to eye, but I know you know what I'm talking about. If you love my son, I mean really love my son, you will see to it that he makes an honest woman out of you, and an honest man of himself. Now go away, and let an old woman rest."

Sam tried to reply, but Becky just waved him away. "Go," she said.

Chapter Thirteen

Sam left but didn't go far. He had a terrible feeling that he should stay close. Audrey followed him into the waiting room.

"Listen, babe," started Sam. "About what my mom said...."

"She's right," answered Audrey. "I know exactly what you do for a living. Maybe not all the details, but I know. I've known for a long time. She's right about something else, too. We can't build a life together if we carry on like this. We have to start being honest with each other. And you have to get a real job."

His Adam's Apple bobbed up and down, as he took a moment to consider.

"Babes," he said at last, "I do love you. And I want to do whatever it takes to make you happy. If it means that much to you, I'll... get out of the business."

He pulled out his phone and scrolled through his contacts, stopping on Alex's number.

"Wait!" said Audrey. "Sam, don't do anything you'll regret, please. Or get us into trouble. I've heard stories. People say it's not easy leaving that world."

Sam chuckled nervously and gave his girlfriend a peck on the lips. "Don't worry, babes. Nobody knows who I am or where I live. Alex handles all that. I'll just... tell him I'm out. That's all."

"Who's Alex? Does *he* know where we live?"

"I never told him, babes, and I never met him at the house. I don't know anything incriminating about him, either. I'll just give him a call and tell him I'm out. Everything will be fine. I promise."

But Sam gulped as he said that, and I could tell he was trying to convince himself, just as much as Audrey.

Alex wasn't happy, to put it mildly. He spent almost the entire phone conversation swearing at Sam, then asking what he was going to tell Joanna (Sam said to tell her to just find someone else), then threatening him with all manner of unpleasantness.

Once all that was over, and Sam convinced Alex that he was leaving the business no matter what, Alex threatened him some more if he was ever reported to the police, and said he never wanted to see Sam again as long as he lived.

"How did it go?" asked Audrey, when Sam had hung up the phone.

"Fine," said Sam, but he was shaking like a leaf. "I think we might have to move, though. Alex said he'd kill me if he ever saw me again."

Audrey gasped. "Babes, are you really sure you want to do this? Are you sure we'll be okay? And what about the money? How are we going to live?"

"We'll be fine," said Sam. "Let's just lay low for a while. Maybe take that holiday we've been thinking about. And don't worry about the money, either. I have a couple hundred grand saved up. Enough to support us for a few years, anyway."

"What do you mean you've..." Audrey started saying, but then stopped herself. She held up her hands in defeat. "Never mind. I don't want to know. We can't leave, though. What about your mother?"

"We'll stick around until she's well enough to come home, and then take her with us."

Audrey folded her arms. "Oh, no we won't. The doctor said she's going to need extra care when she gets out of hospital. Who's going to look after her? Not me, I can promise you that."

Sam tried hard to hide his eye-roll. "Okay, love. We don't have to do anything right now. Let's just think it over for a few days, okay? Right now, I think I need to be with my mother."

"Fine," said Audrey curtly. "But I've had a long day. You stay as long as you need to. I'll grab a ride home and catch some sleep. Will you be okay on your own?"

"Sure," said Sam, and kissed his girlfriend on the lips. "I'll be home later. Bye."

Sometime later, Sam fell asleep in an armchair in his mother's room.

"I know who you are."

My eyes went to the bed; Rebecca was awake. I looked around, but aside from her sleeping son, there was no-one else around.

"Yes, I see you. And I know who you are."

My heart skipped a beat. "H-how...." I started to ask, but then it dawned on me. "Rebecca? Rebecca Martin?"

Rebecca coughed and beckoned me closer with her finger. She gestured towards her sleeping son. "We don't want to wake him."

I moved closer to the old woman, still dumbstruck that she could both see and hear me.

"Years ago," she whispered when I was close enough, "you saved me. My father was a terrible, abusive man, and I almost killed myself over his selfishness. You dragged me back from that precipice."

She reached over and picked up a glass of water from the bedside table, before taking a sip and continuing. "And it wasn't the first time. I first saw you when I was three years old. You protected me for a long time. Then one day, you disappeared."

"But how?" I asked. "How can you see me? Or hear me?"

Rebecca chuckled quietly. "I don't know. My mother always told me I had a guardian angel looking out for me. I suppose I always knew it was you."

I couldn't think of anything better to say, but I knew I should say *something*, so I stammered, "I-I'm sorry for everything that happened to you."

She waved her hand. "Don't be. We all play the hand we're dealt, as the saying goes." She again nodded towards her sleeping son. "I'm dying. No matter what the doctors say. No matter what Sam over there says. But he has his whole life ahead of him. And I need you to protect him. Promise me you'll take care of my boy."

I swallowed hard. As a guardian angel, you can't choose what's going to happen. Where you'll be next. I thought about lying to this woman, promising that everything would be okay. But I couldn't. I knew that Sam was heading for disaster. I would do everything in my power to prevent that, but I just wasn't sure I'd be around long enough to do anything.

Rebecca saw the pain on my face. "That's all right," she said. But she sounded disappointed. "I understand. Perhaps you could promise me something else? Promise me that, when I die, I can be a guardian angel like you."

My chin trembled. I couldn't promise that either, but maybe if I spoke to John, something could be done.

"I'll do my best," I said. Then something occurred to me. "One more thing," I said. "Did you ever make it to Australia?"

Rebecca's eyes glazed over, remembering. "No," she said. "My mother wanted to send me, but I came to my senses. It would've been stupid to go. It wouldn't have changed a thing, but it would've wiped my poor mother out. She would've done anything to keep me happy, but I couldn't let her do that."

After that, she fell asleep.

Rebecca slept peacefully, while Sam continued to snore in the armchair in her room.

Memoirs of a Guardian Angel

About an hour later, Sam woke with a start, to the sound of a long, shrill beep. At first, he didn't know where he was. When he remembered, he saw a long line on the monitor next to his mother's bed. Her EKG was flat-lining.

He shot to his feet and screamed frantically. "Nurse! Nurse! Anyone! Please, come quickly!"

Doctor Deetleefs came racing into the room with two nurses in tow. Despite their soft-soled shoes, their feet pounded on the floor. The doctor took one look at the patient lying on the bed and said, "Sorry, Mister Anderson, but you'll have to leave. We need space to work."

With that, the nurses hurried Sam out of the room.

Sam paced around the waiting area for a full twenty minutes, occasionally rushing to the receptionists to ask if they had any news. Each time, they shook their heads sadly. I could tell Sam was distraught beyond words, and no amount of projecting happy thoughts into his head was going to calm him down.

Finally, the doctor came out of Rebecca's room. Sam rushed up to him, but he had a solemn expression on his face. He put his hand on Sam's arm and said softly, "I'm sorry."

Sam burst into tears and buried his face into the doctor's chest.

Graham Downs

Chapter Fourteen

"I'm so sorry, babe." Audrey held Sam close.

He'd driven back from the hospital in a haze, and it was lucky I'd been there or he'd have had more than a few accidents on the way. Audrey was waiting for him when he got home, and he'd told her everything.

Sam pulled away and sniffed. "Thanks, love," he said. "I'm sorry I'm being such a baby. I'm not the first man to have his mother pass away."

"Nonsense. You loved her. Of course you did. It's why I love you—I don't think I could be with a man who'd be perfectly fine after his mother died."

He smirked at that. "So, what do we do now?"

Audrey hugged him again. "Now, my love, you take some time to mourn. I'll handle the funeral arrangements and everything. I don't want you to worry about anything. I'm here for you, Sam. Always."

Sam ran his hand through his hair. "Oh, crap, the funeral. We need to talk about the funeral. I need to phone the church... which church did she belong to again? I can't even remember. I was raised in that church. I should remember." He started to cry again.

"Relax, babes. I said I'd handle it. Have you got her keys? I'll drive over to her house and see if I can find a contact book, or whatever you call it. Old people still use those, so she must have one, and her pastor or priest or whatever's name should be in there."

"Pastor. It's a pastor. She was Presbyterian. I remember now. She converted after she got pregnant with me, and my father ran off. I think the pastor's name was Rogers, or Robinson, or something like that. And, oh, my father. I have no idea who he is. Do you think he'd want to know?"

She kissed him. "All right, love. I'll see what I can find out. I'll be back as soon as I can. Try and get some rest."

After Audrey left, Sam collapsed on the couch. Myriad thoughts swam through his head. Of his mother, and his childhood, and Audrey. He was going to marry Audrey. If she said yes. But he couldn't ask her now. Maybe after the funeral. What had he done to deserve such a kind, caring woman?

His thoughts were interrupted by the front door bursting open. In stormed Alex, brandishing a pistol.

He pointed it at Sam's head and grinned. "You think I didn't know where you lived, prick? Like I don't do my homework on everyone who works for me?" His smile faded. "All right, bru. It's nothing personal, you understand, my man, but it's time for you to go."

Sam did the weirdest thing, just then. He let his arms drop to his lap, cocked his head back, and stared. Just stared at Alex. I couldn't tell what was going through his mind; his thoughts were too frantic. But he seemed resigned to what was about to happen.

Alex's face took on a confused expression. Still, he didn't hesitate, and as his finger squeezed down on the trigger, I closed my eyes and willed for the gun to jam, or for there to be no bullets in it, or for something, anything to go wrong.

No, I thought. *Not again. Please, not again!*

The gun jammed. Alex couldn't get the trigger to depress. Frustration crept across his face. I smiled.

And then, the familiar feeling came over me. The spiral circled before my eyes. I tried to fight it. *Don't take me away now!* I screamed. But of course, no-one heard me.

The spiral dissipated, leaving me standing in The World Beyond The Veil, with John and Liz staring at me.

"What have I done wrong now?" I asked. The only time I'd ever been brought back here after an assignment, I'd done something I shouldn't've, and was about to be reprimanded.

John and Liz shook with laughter.

"You haven't done anything wrong, silly," said Liz. She was smiling from ear to ear.

John put a hand across her chest. He was practically jumping up and down with excitement. "No, let me tell him."

Liz rolled her eyes. "Oh, okay. If you must."

To say I was confused would've been an understatement. "Tell me what? What's going on?"

"I think it's best if we show you," John put his arm around my shoulders, and gently moved me forward. "Come, there's someone who wants to meet you." He led me into the training room.

"Hello, Adam."

Standing before me was an angel I'd never met before. A female angel. Of course, I could never claim to meet every angel who worked in this place, but there was something about this one.

I looked at her, then at John, then at Liz. They were all smiling.

"Adam," said John. "This is Ricky."

She held out her hand. "Pleased to finally make your acquaintance."

When I didn't respond, all three of them burst out laughing. And then I saw it. Looking at her, I could see the cute little three-year-old girl, the rebellious thirteen-year-old, the noble, dignified old woman on her death-bed. Finally, I managed to speak.

"B-but how? Why?"

It was Ricky who answered. "I'm not really sure. I couldn't remember anything when I arrived, but then John met me inside the gates. He said you made me a promise back there. He told me I asked if I could be a guardian angel, and you said you'd see what you could do. Well, you did it. Here I am."

"Well, Adam, looks like you've got yourself a protégé," said Liz. She giggled. "Good luck!"

"No," I said, quickly. "I mean, I can't. I've only just started doing this myself. How could I possibly teach someone else?"

"You don't have to, Adam." John stepped forward and gave Liz a disparaging look. "You're a guardian angel, not a trainer. That's my job." He turned to Ricky. "That is, if she'll have me, I'd love to train her. You go back to your job. I'll do mine."

With that, the spirals started again. Where was I off to this time?

Epilogue

People often say they have a guardian angel looking out for them, especially when they survive a harrowing experience, like almost crashing their cars, falling off ladders, or choking on pieces of chewing gum. After a near-catastrophe like that, how often have you thought, "Wow, my guardian angel must be really looking out for me today?"

But I wonder how many people actually believe it to be true. There aren't many people who talk openly about their guardian angel when things are going well... are there?

My name is Ricky, and I am a guardian angel.

Graham Downs

Acknowledgements

First off, and most importantly, a huge thank you to my wife, Elmari, for putting up with all my issues, and listening to me ramble on and on about this book. It's taken me a long time to write (almost two years!), and her support has been unwavering. She was the first person to read *Memoirs* after I was done, but long before it was anywhere near ready for publication. She didn't pull any punches in her feedback, and the story is a million times better because of it.

Thanks, as well, to the rest of my family, whose continued support and encouragement are things I should never take for granted. These people are always willing to read for me, and their insights never cease to amaze.

To my wonderful readers, thank you for picking up this book. I know clicking that "Buy" button is a big step and a tough decision. I love every single one of you, and I appreciate you reading this far from the bottom of my heart!

The cover for this book was designed by the wonderfully talented Tallulah Habib from *Covers by Tallulah*. To see her work, take a look at her website, http://tallulahlucy.com/cover-designs/. She doesn't just do covers, either.

Finally, to my writing group on Facebook, *The Dragon Writers*. I've learnt so much from every single one of you, and when I'm feeling down, or have a bit of writer's block, I know I can always pop into the group for some encouragement, or even just a pick-me-up. Even if I don't Like or comment on your posts, I hope you all realise just how much your community means to me.

About the Author

Graham Downs is a South African author of short stories, flash fiction, and novelettes, in a variety of genres. *Memoirs of a Guardian Angel* is his longest work to date.

He currently lives in Alberton, Gauteng, with his wife and their dog, Becky. He spends a good portion of his free time reading and, as with his writing, he reads books in a huge range of genres and lengths. He's also passionate about South African authors—particularly independently published ones.

If you want to keep up with Graham's writing journey, you can sign up for his e-mail newsletter at https://www.grahamdowns.co.za/. You'll get a free book if you do.

Please Review

Reviews are the lifeblood of an author, especially a self-published one. They help other readers find books that might interest them, and open the door to loads of marketing opportunities.

So if you enjoyed this book, the author would greatly appreciate it if you'd return to the place where you bought it, and write a few words explaining what you thought.

Your review doesn't need to be an essay—although it can be as long as you want it to be. Just a few sentences describing whether you liked it or not are just fine.

If you're really uncomfortable writing anything, you can also simply rate the book (from one to five stars) on social reading site Goodreads, without necessarily writing a review.

If you have the Goodreads app installed on your iOS or Android device, simply use it to scan the barcode on the back cover of this book.

Also by Graham Downs

Stingers

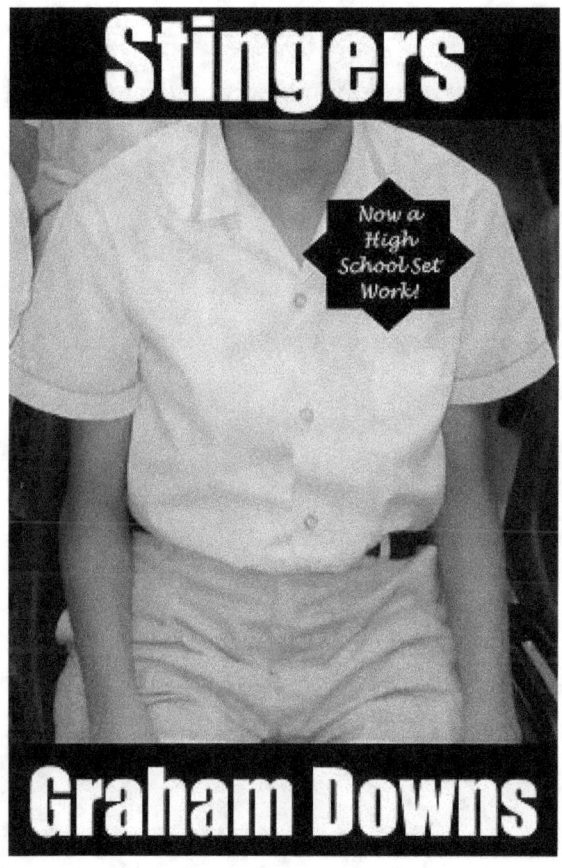

Thirteen year old James Clarke is always being picked on in school. He hates sports, and he particularly hates Stingers, a schoolyard game in which children throw tennis balls at each other. The other kids always seem to throw the ball harder, when it's at him. His physical education teacher, Mr Evans, has no sympathy for the boy, believing he just needs to toughen up a bit.

When James returns home from school after a rough game of Stingers, his mother is mortified when she sees the bruises on his arm and chest. She phones the school to try and put a stop to the cruel bullying of her son.

But her phone call only makes things worse, as the bullying escalates to levels that nobody imagined possible.

Heaven and Earth: Paranormal Flash Fiction

"There are more things in heaven and earth, Horatio, Than are dreamt of in your philosophy."
- Hamlet (1.5.167-8)

Demons, witches, extra-sensory perception, possessed animals, and an ever-loving God. There is much that exists, or is claimed to exist, in the world today, that we are yet to understand.

A perfect introduction into the inner workings of the weird mind of Graham Downs, this collection of flash fiction paranormal stories contains:

•The Thing in the Window,

•An Automatic Decision,

•Telepathic Link,

•The Witch of Wellington, and

•The Christmas Bird.

All have been newly edited and polished since publication on his website in 2014, and some with new endings.

It also contains the never-before published story, Under the Sheets, about an old woman who believes she is being haunted by a strange ghost, living under her bed.

Heritage of Deceit

While surfing the Internet at work, Lloyd believes he's found a relic from an old genocide. If he's right, the artefact would be worth a ton of money, and it will give lots of people closure when they find out what really happened to their families.

But there's one problem. The artefact—if it really exists—is in the possession of Carla, a shy woman in the company's Accounts Department, and she never lets it out of her sight.

Lloyd seeks the help of his friend and fellow employee, Robert, whom Carla is desperately in love with. Will Robert agree to use Carla's feelings for him to get information about the mysterious object?

Billy's Zombie

Young Billy MacIntyre has always been a weird kid, always taking every little slight to heart.

One day, he decides that he's had enough of the relentless

mocking and bullying at school and around town.

He decides to exact his revenge on all those simpletons who have done him wrong. And he does it by taking a book of Necromancy out of the library, and raising a zombie from the dead!

www.ingramcontent.com/pod-product-compliance
Lightning Source LLC
Chambersburg PA
CBHW051549280626
47162CB00021B/1648